geeky f@b 5

Lucy

Zara

Marina

A.J.

Sofia

Hubble

PAPERCUT Z ™

MORE GREAT GRAPHIC NOVEL SERIES AVAILABLE FROM PAPERCUTZ

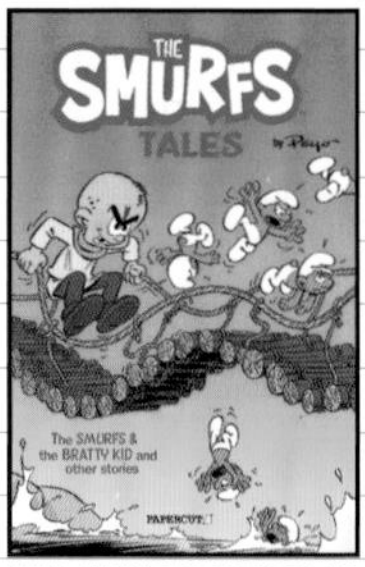
THE SMURFS
TALES
The SMURFS & the BRATTY KID and other stories
PAPERCUTZ
THE SMURFS TALES #1

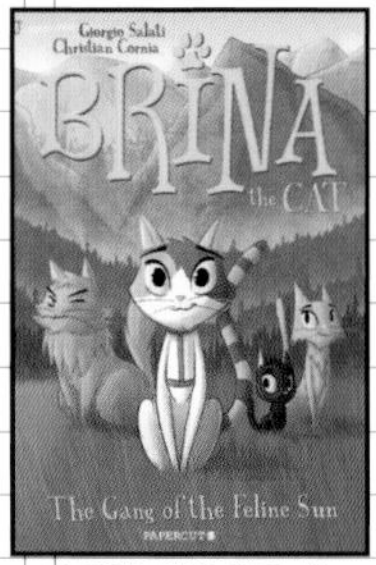
Giorgio Salati
Christian Cornia
BRINA
the CAT
The Gang of the Feline Sun
PAPERCUTZ
BRINA THE CAT #1

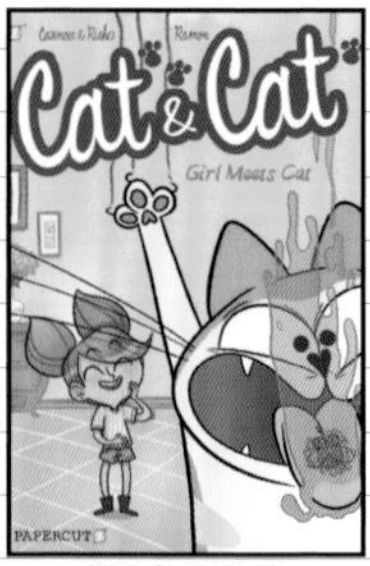
Cat & Cat
Girl Meets Cat
PAPERCUTZ
CAT & CAT #1

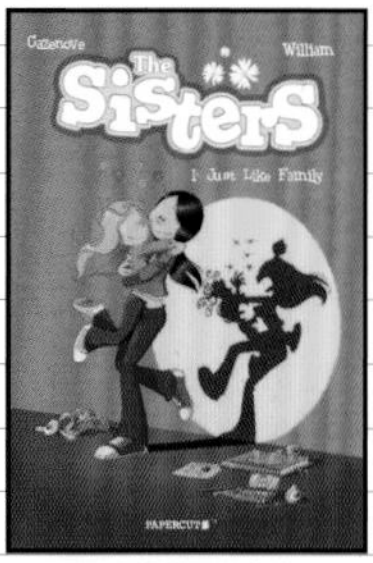
Cazenove
William
The Sisters
PAPERCUTZ
THE SISTERS #1

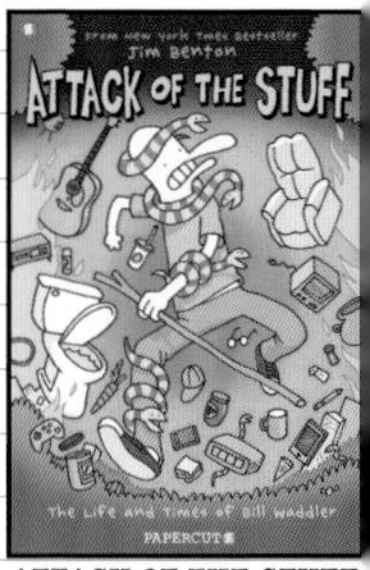
Jim Benton
ATTACK OF THE STUFF
The Life and Times of Bill Waddler
PAPERCUTZ
ATTACK OF THE STUFF

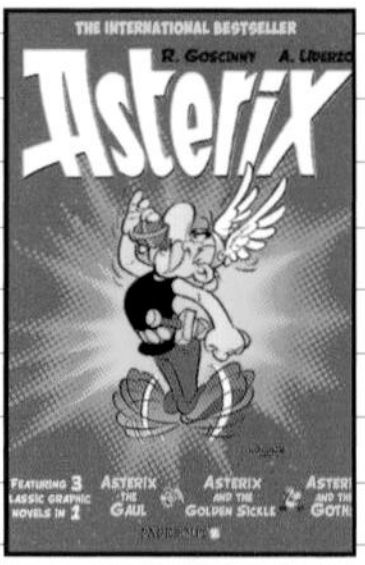
THE INTERNATIONAL BESTSELLER
R. GOSCINNY
Asterix
PAPERCUTZ
ASTERIX #1

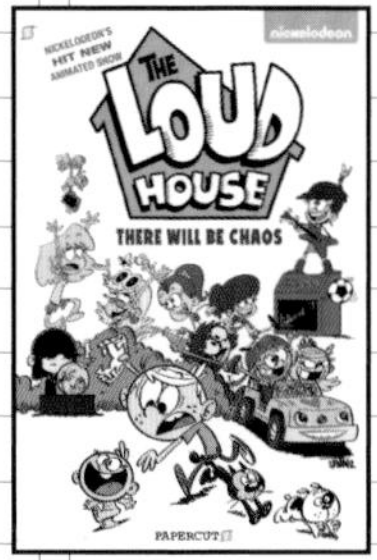
nickelodeon
THE LOUD HOUSE
THERE WILL BE CHAOS
PAPERCUTZ
THE LOUD HOUSE #1

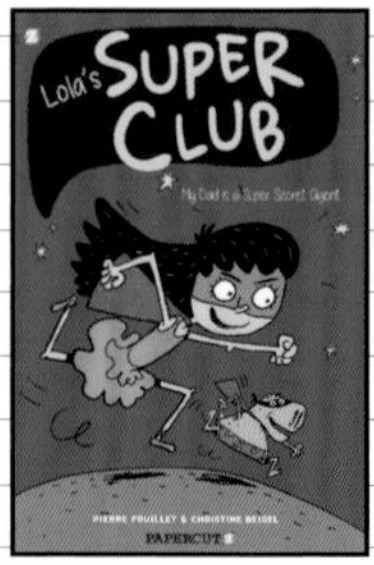
Lola's SUPER CLUB
PIERRE FOUILLET & CHRISTINE BEIGEL
PAPERCUTZ
LOLA'S SUPER CLUB #1

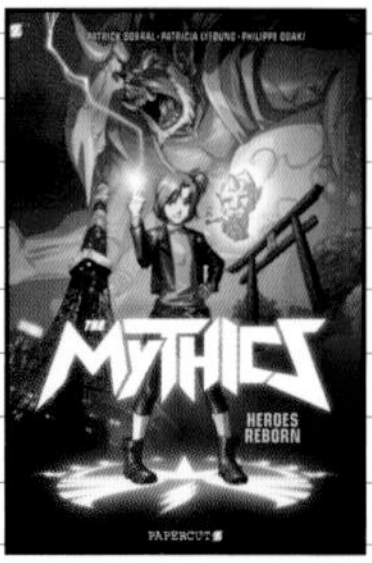
THE MYTHICS
HEROES REBORN
PAPERCUTZ
THE MYTHICS #1

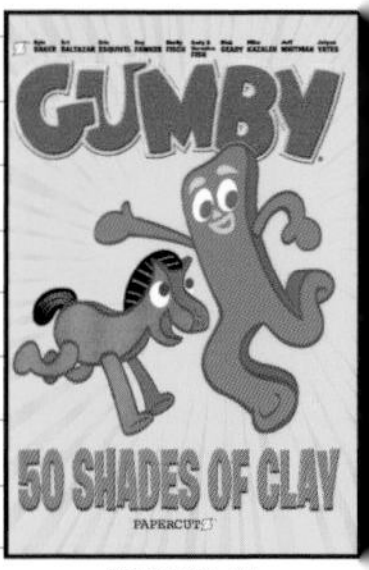
GUMBY
50 SHADES OF CLAY
PAPERCUTZ
GUMBY #1

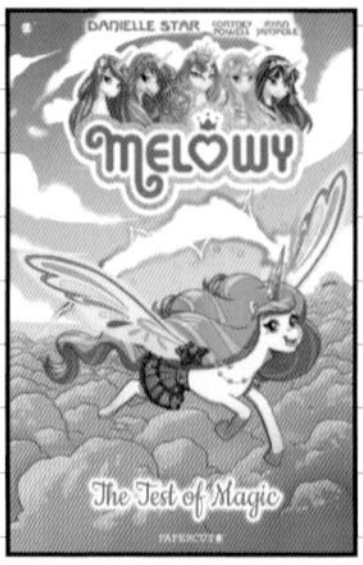
DANIELLE STAR
Melowy
The Test of Magic
PAPERCUTZ
MELOWY #1

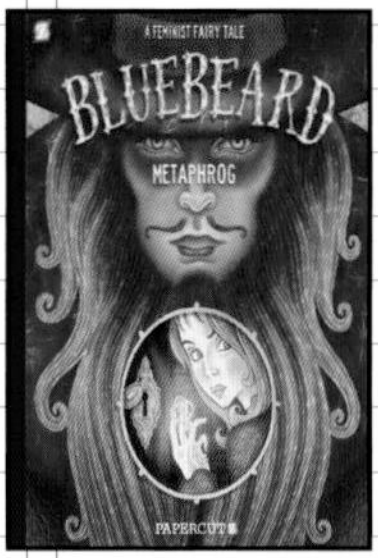
A FEMINIST FAIRY TALE
BLUEBEARD
METAPHROG
PAPERCUTZ
BLUEBEARD

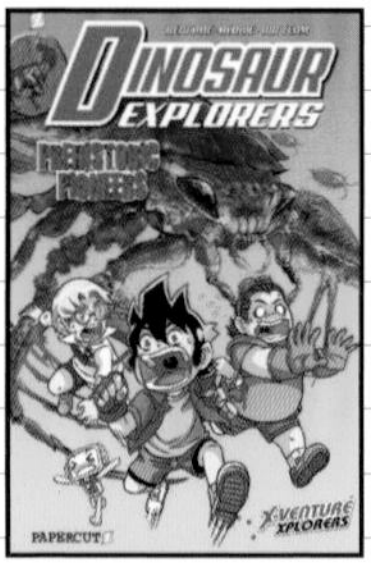
DINOSAUR EXPLORERS
PAPERCUTZ
DINOSAUR EXPLORERS #1

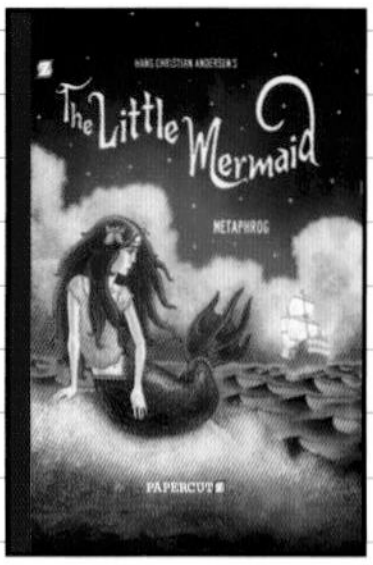
HANS CHRISTIAN ANDERSEN'S
The Little Mermaid
METAPHROG
PAPERCUTZ
THE LITTLE MERMAID

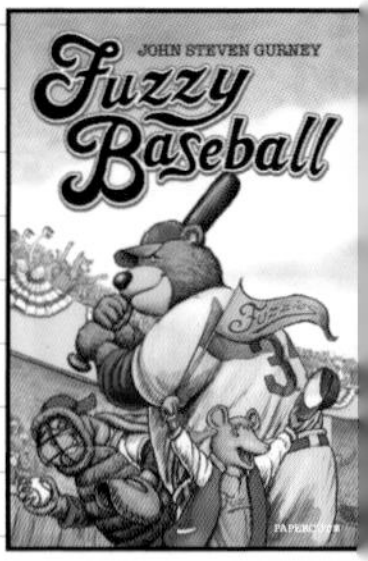
JOHN STEVEN GURNEY
Fuzzy Baseball
PAPERCUTZ
FUZZY BASEBALL #1

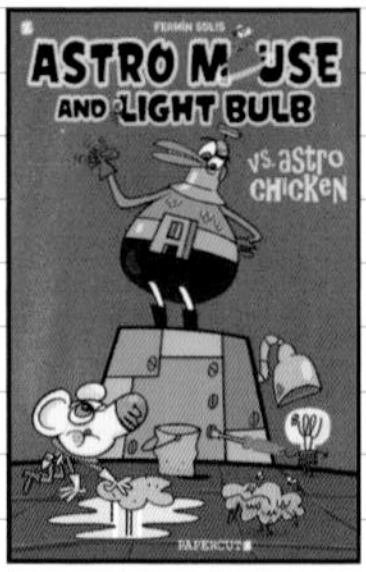
FERMÍN SOLÍS
ASTRO MOUSE AND LIGHT BULB
vs. astro chicken
PAPERCUTZ
ASTRO MOUSE AND LIGHT BULB #1

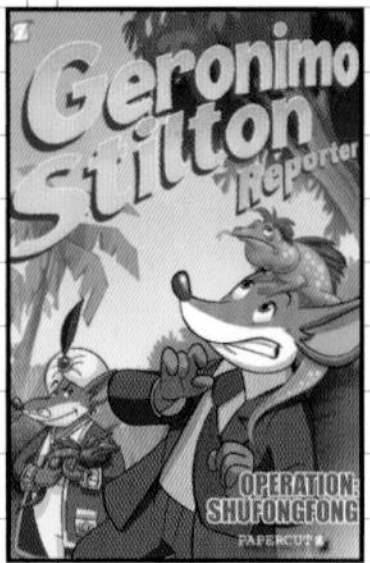
Geronimo Stilton
Reporter
OPERATION: SHUFONGFONG
PAPERCUTZ
GERONIMO STILTON REPORTER #1

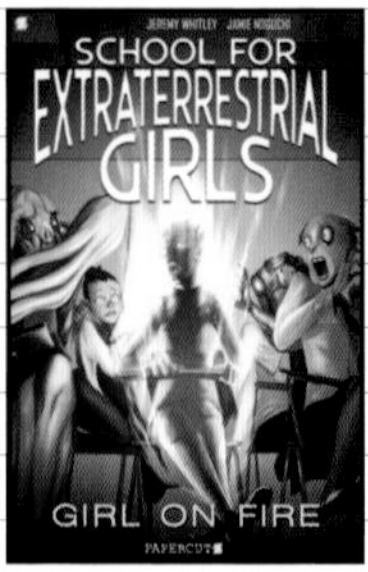
JEREMY WHITLEY · JAMIE NOGUCHI
SCHOOL FOR EXTRATERRESTRIAL GIRLS
GIRL ON FIRE
PAPERCUTZ
SCHOOL FOR EXTRA-TERRESTRIAL GIRLS #1

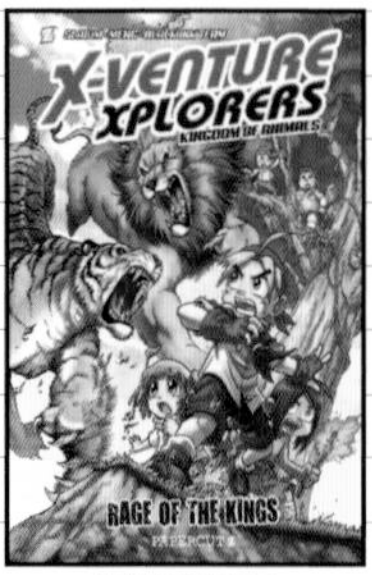
X-VENTURE XPLORERS
KINGDOM OF ANIMALS
RAGE OF THE KINGS
PAPERCUTZ
X-VENTURE XPLORERS #1

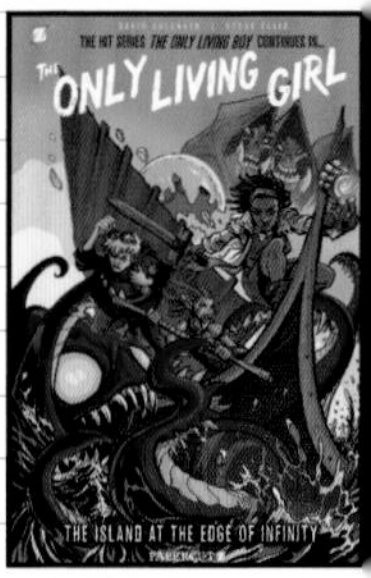
THE ONLY LIVING GIRL
THE ISLAND AT THE EDGE OF INFINITY
PAPERCUTZ
THE ONLY LIVING GIRL #1

papercutz.com
Also available where ebooks are sold.

geeky f@b 5 ®

#5 "Smoky Mountain Science Squad"

LUCY & LIZ LAREAU — Writers
RYAN JAMPOLE — Artist

PAPERCUTZ™
NEW YORK

geeky f@b 5®

#5 "Smoky Mountain Science Squad"

LUCY & LIZ LAREAU—Writers
RYAN JAMPOLE—Artist
LAURIE E. SMITH—Colorist
WILSON RAMOS JR.—Letterer
JENNIFER HERNANDEZ—Cover Artist
JEFF WHITMAN—Managing Editor
JIM SALICRUP
Editor-in-Chief

papercutz.com
geekyfabfive.com

Hardcover ISBN 978-1-5458-0562-6
Paperback ISBN 978-1-5458-0561-9

Printed in Turkey Elma Basım
June 2021

Papercutz books may be purchased for business or promotional use. For information on bulk purchases, please contact Macmillan Corporate and Premium Sales Department at (800) 221-7945 x5442.

Distributed by Macmillan
First Printing

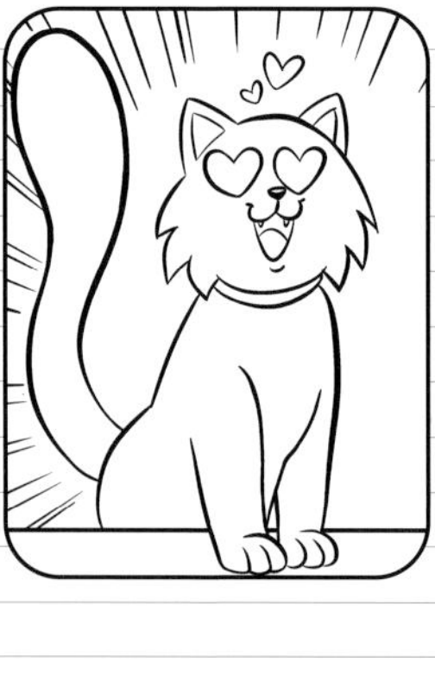

Teacher's Guide available at:
http://papercutz.com/educator-resources-papercutz

CHAPTER ONE: LAZY SUMMER DAYS

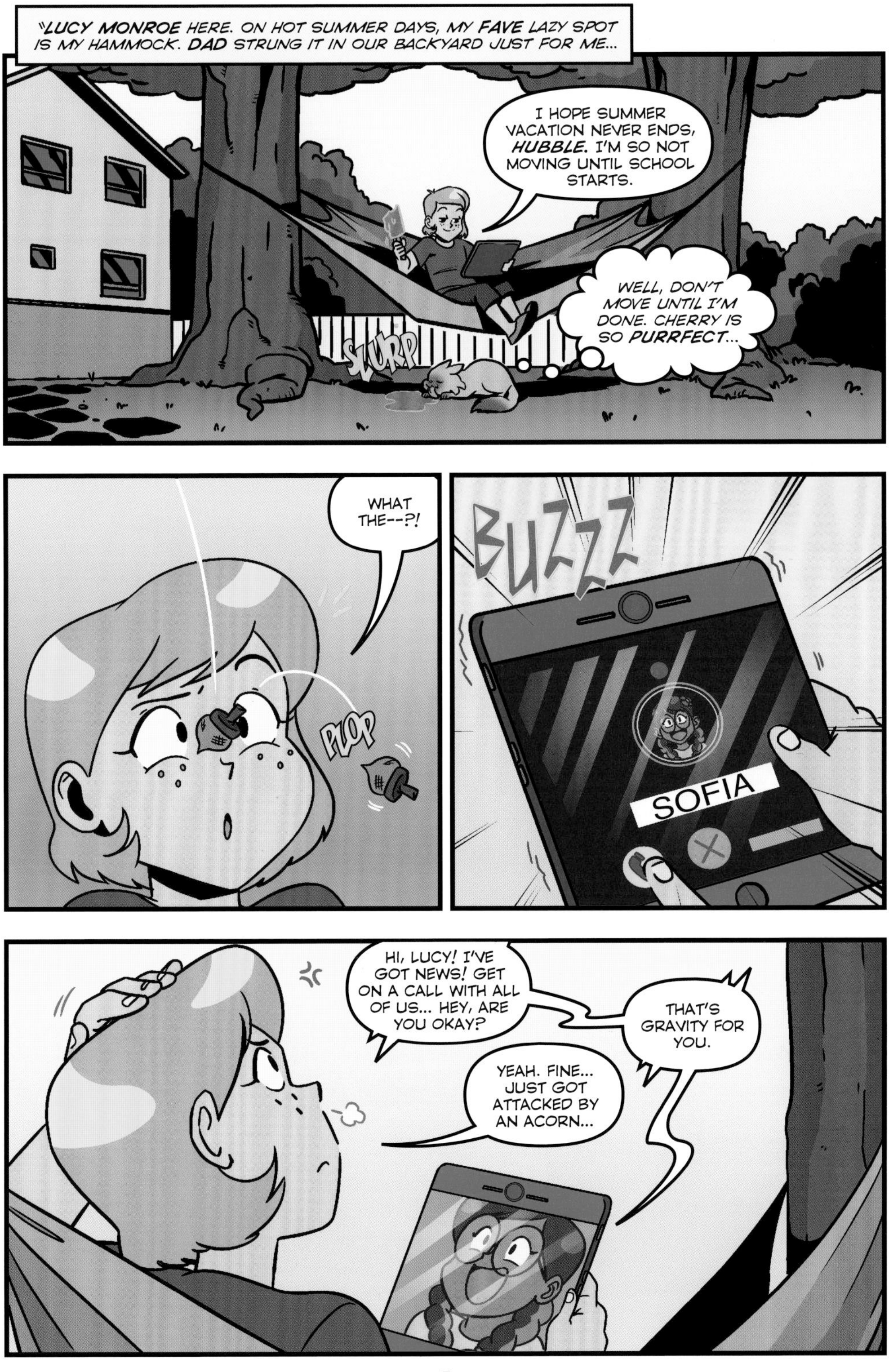

"LUCY MONROE HERE. ON HOT SUMMER DAYS, MY FAVE LAZY SPOT IS MY HAMMOCK. DAD STRUNG IT IN OUR BACKYARD JUST FOR ME...
I HOPE SUMMER VACATION NEVER ENDS, HUBBLE. I'M SO NOT MOVING UNTIL SCHOOL STARTS.
WELL, DON'T MOVE UNTIL I'M DONE. CHERRY IS SO PURRFECT...
SLURP
WHAT THE--?!
PLOP
BUZZZ
SOFIA
HI, LUCY! I'VE GOT NEWS! GET ON A CALL WITH ALL OF US... HEY, ARE YOU OKAY?
THAT'S GRAVITY FOR YOU.
YEAH. FINE... JUST GOT ATTACKED BY AN ACORN...

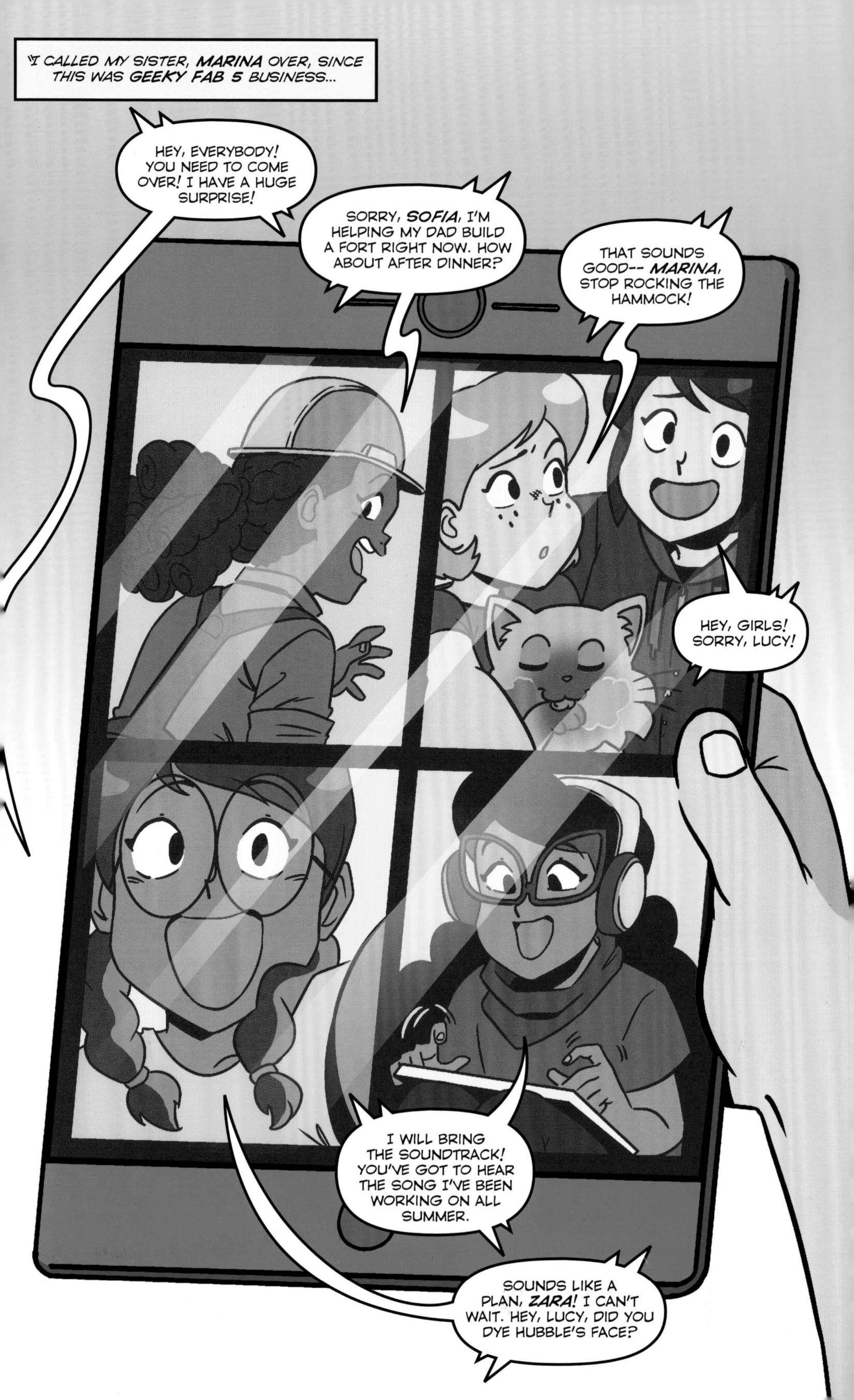

"I CALLED MY SISTER, MARINA OVER, SINCE THIS WAS GEEKY FAB 5 BUSINESS...
HEY, EVERYBODY! YOU NEED TO COME OVER! I HAVE A HUGE SURPRISE!
SORRY, SOFIA, I'M HELPING MY DAD BUILD A FORT RIGHT NOW. HOW ABOUT AFTER DINNER?
THAT SOUNDS GOOD-- MARINA, STOP ROCKING THE HAMMOCK!
HEY, GIRLS! SORRY, LUCY!
I WILL BRING THE SOUNDTRACK! YOU'VE GOT TO HEAR THE SONG I'VE BEEN WORKING ON ALL SUMMER.
SOUNDS LIKE A PLAN, ZARA! I CAN'T WAIT. HEY, LUCY, DID YOU DYE HUBBLE'S FACE?

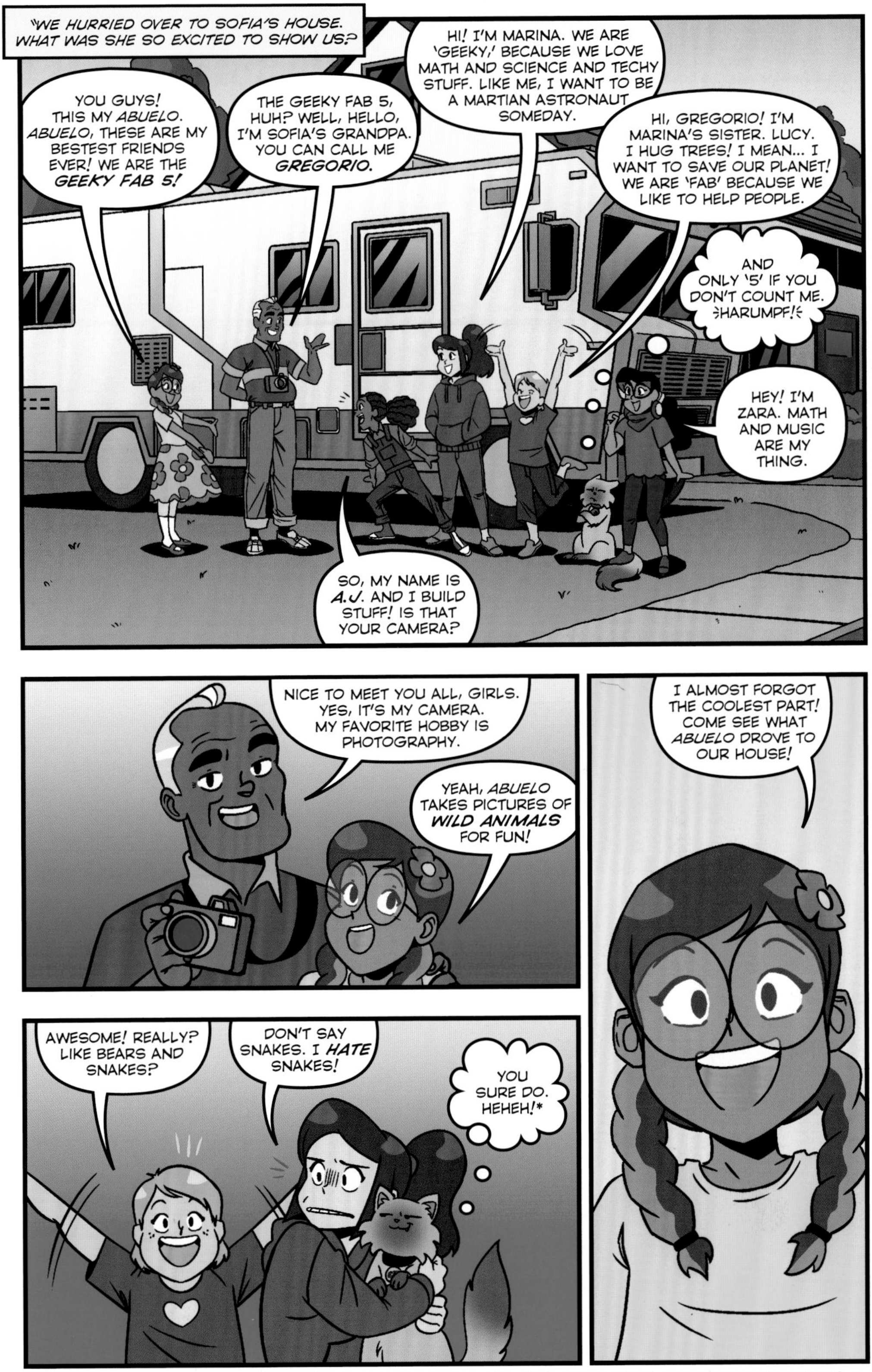
"WE HURRIED OVER TO SOFIA'S HOUSE. WHAT WAS SHE SO EXCITED TO SHOW US?
YOU GUYS! THIS MY ABUELO. ABUELO, THESE ARE MY BESTEST FRIENDS EVER! WE ARE THE GEEKY FAB 5!
THE GEEKY FAB 5, HUH? WELL, HELLO, I'M SOFIA'S GRANDPA. YOU CAN CALL ME GREGORIO.
HI! I'M MARINA. WE ARE 'GEEKY,' BECAUSE WE LOVE MATH AND SCIENCE AND TECHY STUFF. LIKE ME, I WANT TO BE A MARTIAN ASTRONAUT SOMEDAY.
HI, GREGORIO! I'M MARINA'S SISTER. LUCY. I HUG TREES! I MEAN... I WANT TO SAVE OUR PLANET! WE ARE 'FAB' BECAUSE WE LIKE TO HELP PEOPLE.
AND ONLY '5' IF YOU DON'T COUNT ME. HARUMPF!
HEY! I'M ZARA. MATH AND MUSIC ARE MY THING.
SO, MY NAME IS A.J. AND I BUILD STUFF! IS THAT YOUR CAMERA?
NICE TO MEET YOU ALL, GIRLS. YES, IT'S MY CAMERA. MY FAVORITE HOBBY IS PHOTOGRAPHY.
YEAH, ABUELO TAKES PICTURES OF WILD ANIMALS FOR FUN!
I ALMOST FORGOT THE COOLEST PART! COME SEE WHAT ABUELO DROVE TO OUR HOUSE!
AWESOME! REALLY? LIKE BEARS AND SNAKES?
DON'T SAY SNAKES. I HATE SNAKES!
YOU SURE DO. HEHEH!*

*CHECK OUT GEEKY FAB FIVE #3 "DOGGONE CATASTROPHE" AND FIND OUT WHAT A NAUGHTY KITTY HUBBLE IS...

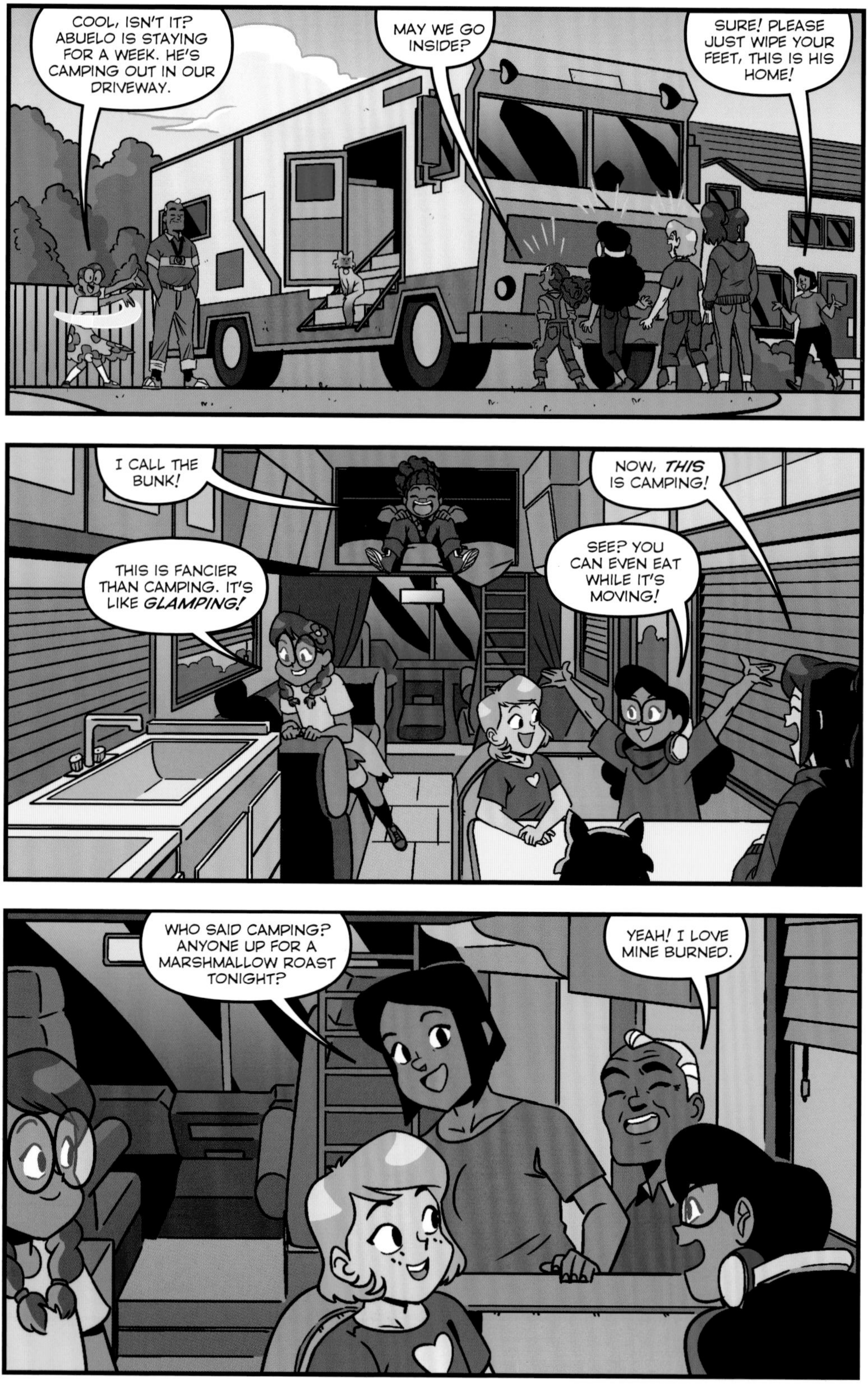
COOL, ISN'T IT? ABUELO IS STAYING FOR A WEEK. HE'S CAMPING OUT IN OUR DRIVEWAY.
MAY WE GO INSIDE?
SURE! PLEASE JUST WIPE YOUR FEET, THIS IS HIS HOME!
I CALL THE BUNK!
NOW, *THIS* IS CAMPING!
THIS IS FANCIER THAN CAMPING. IT'S LIKE *GLAMPING!*
SEE? YOU CAN EVEN EAT WHILE IT'S MOVING!
WHO SAID CAMPING? ANYONE UP FOR A MARSHMALLOW ROAST TONIGHT?
YEAH! I LOVE MINE BURNED.

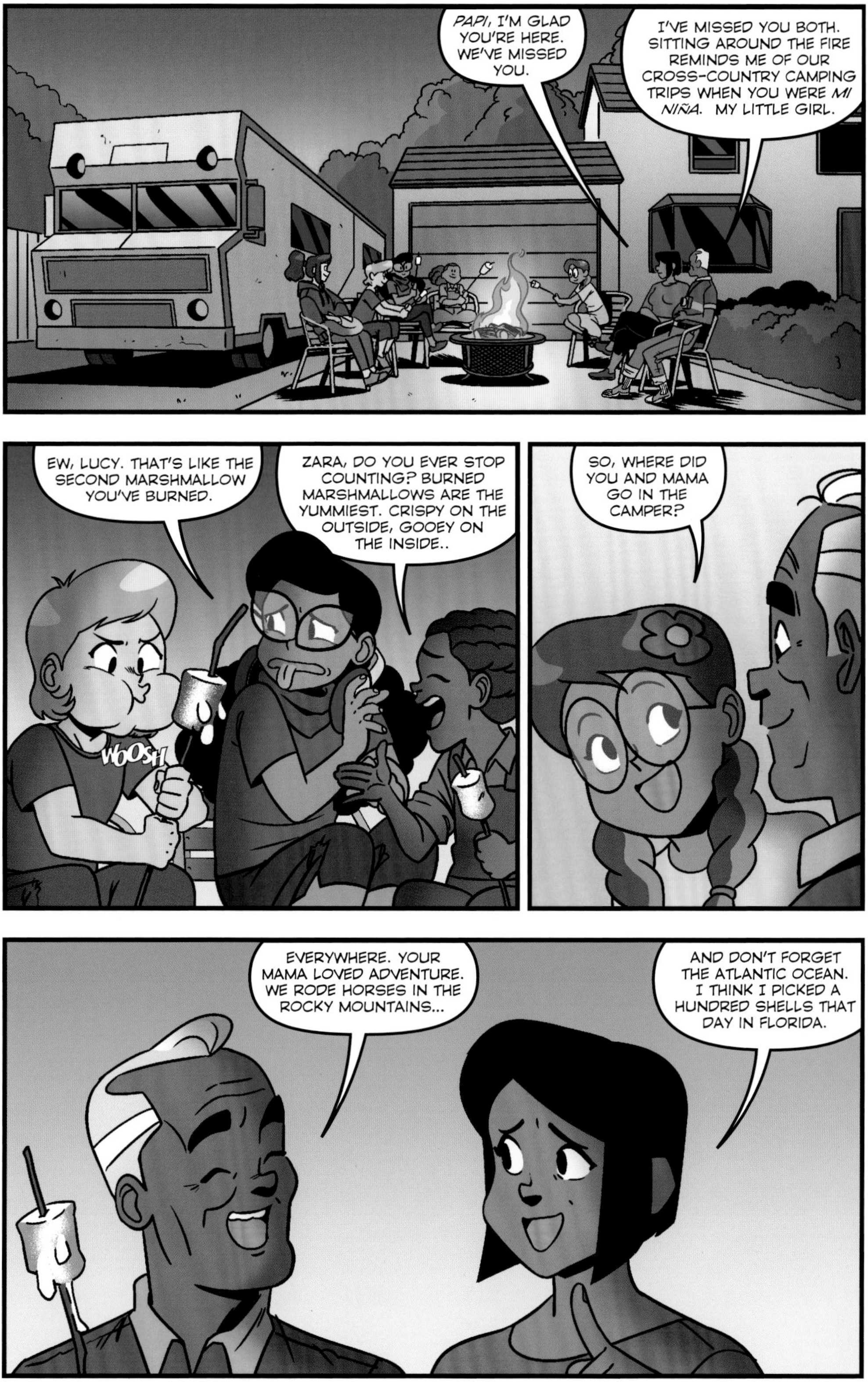
PAPI, I'M GLAD YOU'RE HERE. WE'VE MISSED YOU.
I'VE MISSED YOU BOTH. SITTING AROUND THE FIRE REMINDS ME OF OUR CROSS-COUNTRY CAMPING TRIPS WHEN YOU WERE *MI NIÑA*. MY LITTLE GIRL.
EW, LUCY. THAT'S LIKE THE SECOND MARSHMALLOW YOU'VE BURNED.
ZARA, DO YOU EVER STOP COUNTING? BURNED MARSHMALLOWS ARE THE YUMMIEST. CRISPY ON THE OUTSIDE, GOOEY ON THE INSIDE..
WOOSH
SO, WHERE DID YOU AND MAMA GO IN THE CAMPER?
EVERYWHERE. YOUR MAMA LOVED ADVENTURE. WE RODE HORSES IN THE ROCKY MOUNTAINS...
AND DON'T FORGET THE ATLANTIC OCEAN. I THINK I PICKED A HUNDRED SHELLS THAT DAY IN FLORIDA.

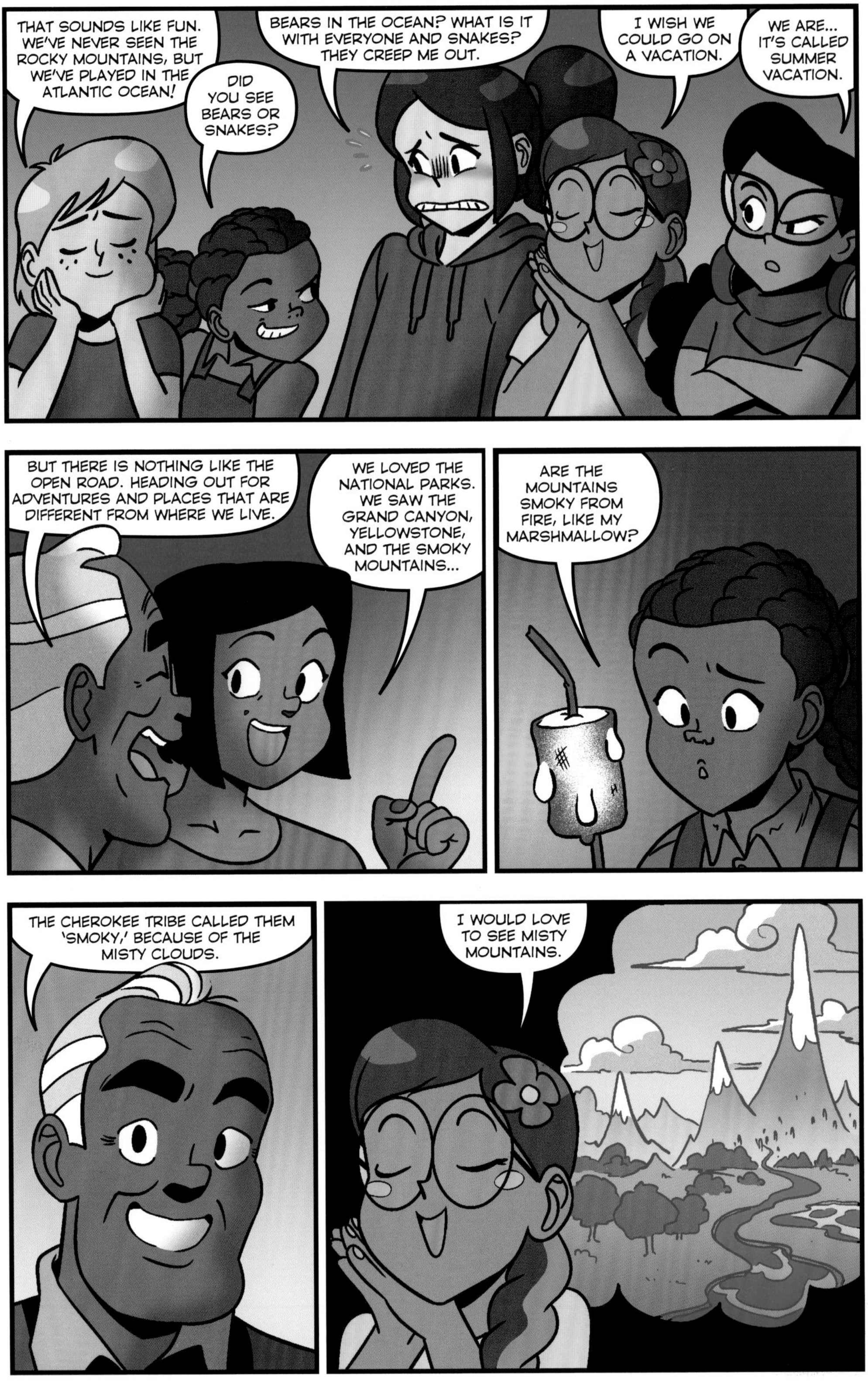
THAT SOUNDS LIKE FUN. WE'VE NEVER SEEN THE ROCKY MOUNTAINS, BUT WE'VE PLAYED IN THE ATLANTIC OCEAN!
DID YOU SEE BEARS OR SNAKES?
BEARS IN THE OCEAN? WHAT IS IT WITH EVERYONE AND SNAKES? THEY CREEP ME OUT.
I WISH WE COULD GO ON A VACATION.
WE ARE... IT'S CALLED SUMMER VACATION.
BUT THERE IS NOTHING LIKE THE OPEN ROAD. HEADING OUT FOR ADVENTURES AND PLACES THAT ARE DIFFERENT FROM WHERE WE LIVE.
WE LOVED THE NATIONAL PARKS. WE SAW THE GRAND CANYON, YELLOWSTONE, AND THE SMOKY MOUNTAINS...
ARE THE MOUNTAINS SMOKY FROM FIRE, LIKE MY MARSHMALLOW?
THE CHEROKEE TRIBE CALLED THEM 'SMOKY,' BECAUSE OF THE MISTY CLOUDS.
I WOULD LOVE TO SEE MISTY MOUNTAINS.

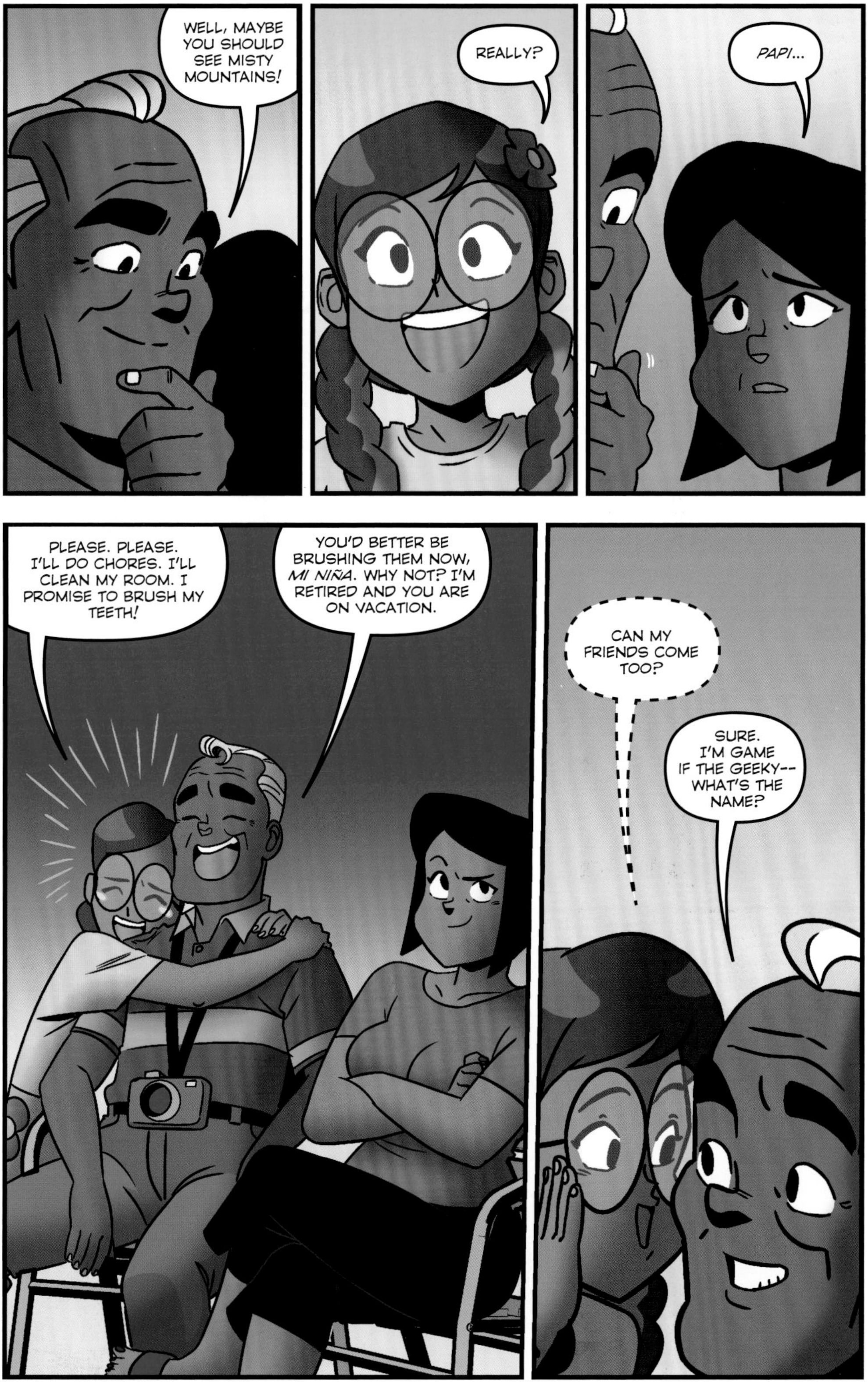
WELL, MAYBE YOU SHOULD SEE MISTY MOUNTAINS!
REALLY?
PAPI...
PLEASE. PLEASE. I'LL DO CHORES. I'LL CLEAN MY ROOM. I PROMISE TO BRUSH MY TEETH!
YOU'D BETTER BE BRUSHING THEM NOW, *MI NIÑA*. WHY NOT? I'M RETIRED AND YOU ARE ON VACATION.
CAN MY FRIENDS COME TOO?
SURE. I'M GAME IF THE GEEKY-- WHAT'S THE NAME?

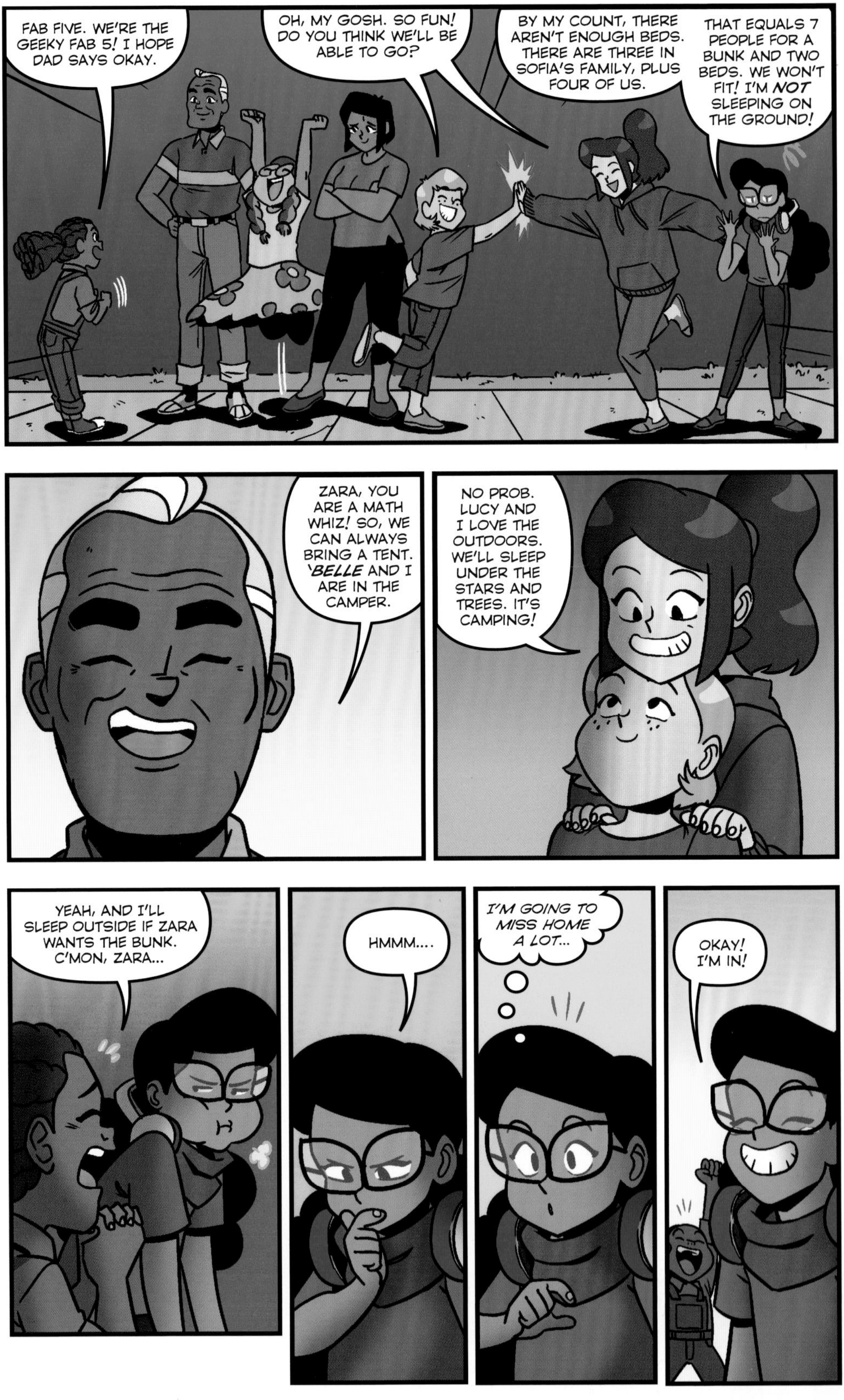
FAB FIVE. WE'RE THE GEEKY FAB 5! I HOPE DAD SAYS OKAY.
OH, MY GOSH. SO FUN! DO YOU THINK WE'LL BE ABLE TO GO?
BY MY COUNT, THERE AREN'T ENOUGH BEDS. THERE ARE THREE IN SOFIA'S FAMILY, PLUS FOUR OF US.
THAT EQUALS 7 PEOPLE FOR A BUNK AND TWO BEDS. WE WON'T FIT! I'M NOT SLEEPING ON THE GROUND!
ZARA, YOU ARE A MATH WHIZ! SO, WE CAN ALWAYS BRING A TENT. 'BELLE AND I ARE IN THE CAMPER.
NO PROB. LUCY AND I LOVE THE OUTDOORS. WE'LL SLEEP UNDER THE STARS AND TREES. IT'S CAMPING!
YEAH, AND I'LL SLEEP OUTSIDE IF ZARA WANTS THE BUNK. C'MON, ZARA...
HMMM....
I'M GOING TO MISS HOME A LOT...
OKAY! I'M IN!

CHAPTER TWO: ROADTRIPPIN'

"WITH OUR PARENT'S PERMISSION, WE KICKED INTO PACKING, PLANNING, AND YES, CLEANING MODE. WE WERE LEAVING IN A WEEK AND WE WERE SO EXCITED TO VISIT OUR FIRST NATIONAL PARK!

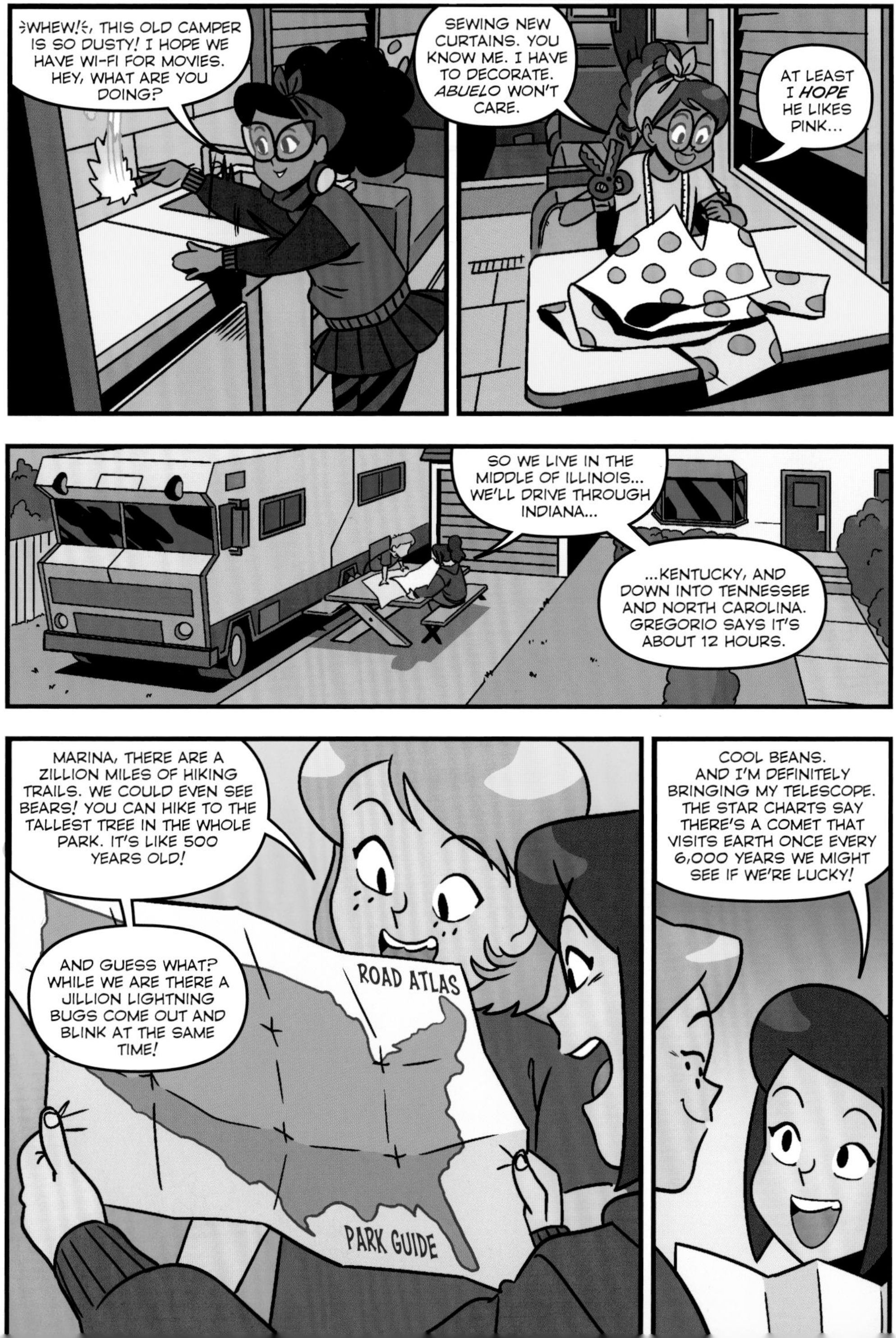

WHEW!, THIS OLD CAMPER IS SO DUSTY! I HOPE WE HAVE WI-FI FOR MOVIES. HEY, WHAT ARE YOU DOING?
SEWING NEW CURTAINS. YOU KNOW ME. I HAVE TO DECORATE. ABUELO WON'T CARE.
AT LEAST I HOPE HE LIKES PINK...
SO WE LIVE IN THE MIDDLE OF ILLINOIS... WE'LL DRIVE THROUGH INDIANA...
...KENTUCKY, AND DOWN INTO TENNESSEE AND NORTH CAROLINA. GREGORIO SAYS IT'S ABOUT 12 HOURS.
MARINA, THERE ARE A ZILLION MILES OF HIKING TRAILS. WE COULD EVEN SEE BEARS! YOU CAN HIKE TO THE TALLEST TREE IN THE WHOLE PARK. IT'S LIKE 500 YEARS OLD!
AND GUESS WHAT? WHILE WE ARE THERE A JILLION LIGHTNING BUGS COME OUT AND BLINK AT THE SAME TIME!
ROAD ATLAS
PARK GUIDE
COOL BEANS. AND I'M DEFINITELY BRINGING MY TELESCOPE. THE STAR CHARTS SAY THERE'S A COMET THAT VISITS EARTH ONCE EVERY 6,000 YEARS WE MIGHT SEE IF WE'RE LUCKY!

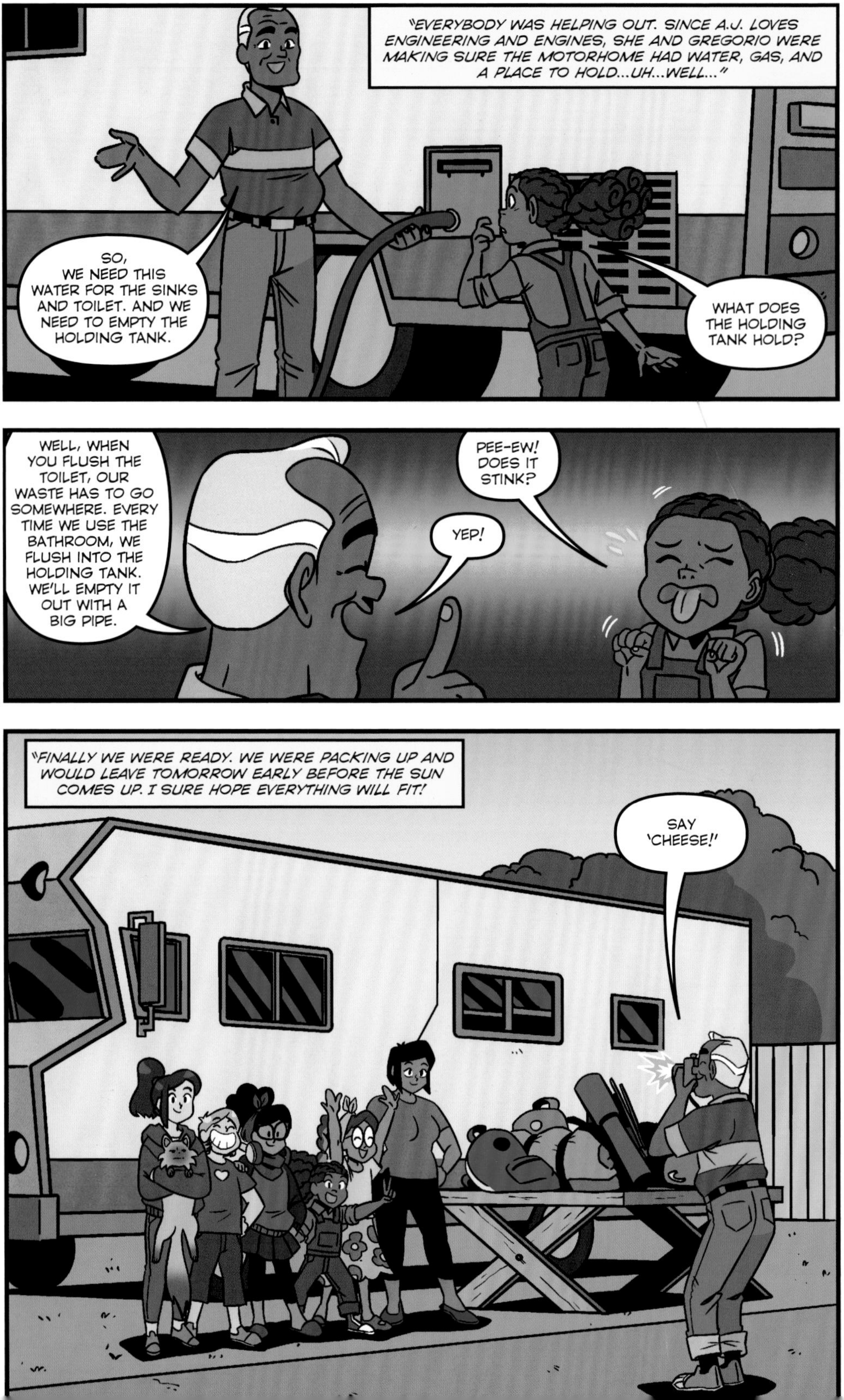
"EVERYBODY WAS HELPING OUT. SINCE A.J. LOVES ENGINEERING AND ENGINES, SHE AND GREGORIO WERE MAKING SURE THE MOTORHOME HAD WATER, GAS, AND A PLACE TO HOLD...UH...WELL..."
SO, WE NEED THIS WATER FOR THE SINKS AND TOILET. AND WE NEED TO EMPTY THE HOLDING TANK.
WHAT DOES THE HOLDING TANK HOLD?
WELL, WHEN YOU FLUSH THE TOILET, OUR WASTE HAS TO GO SOMEWHERE. EVERY TIME WE USE THE BATHROOM, WE FLUSH INTO THE HOLDING TANK. WE'LL EMPTY IT OUT WITH A BIG PIPE.
PEE-EW! DOES IT STINK?
YEP!
"FINALLY WE WERE READY. WE WERE PACKING UP AND WOULD LEAVE TOMORROW EARLY BEFORE THE SUN COMES UP. I SURE HOPE EVERYTHING WILL FIT!
SAY 'CHEESE!'

CHAPTER THREE: ON THE ROAD

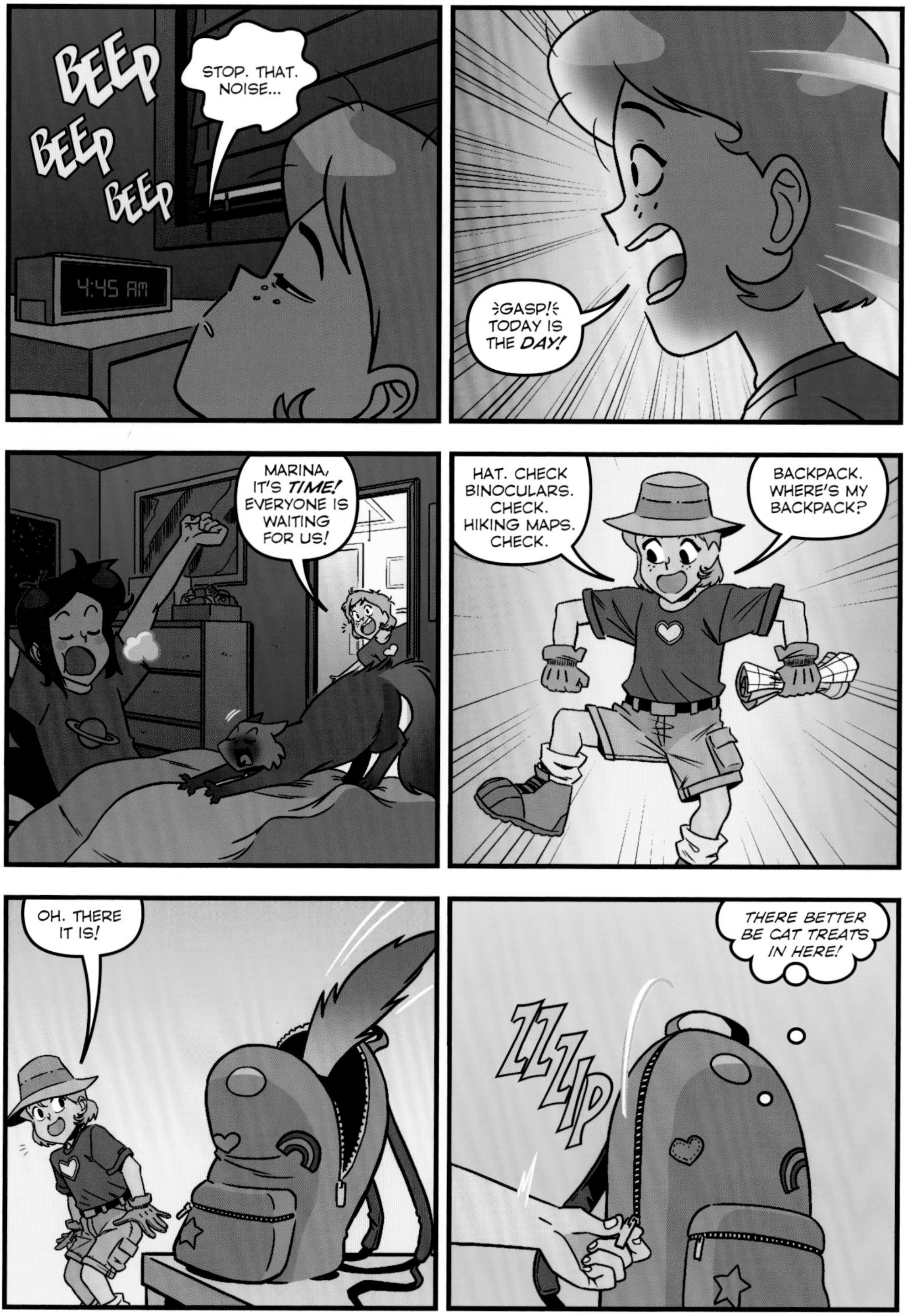
BEEP
BEEP
BEEP
STOP. THAT. NOISE...
4:45 AM
GASP! TODAY IS THE *DAY!*
MARINA, IT'S *TIME!* EVERYONE IS WAITING FOR US!
HAT. CHECK BINOCULARS. CHECK. HIKING MAPS. CHECK.
BACKPACK. WHERE'S MY BACKPACK?
OH. THERE IT IS!
ZZZIP
THERE BETTER BE CAT TREATS IN HERE!

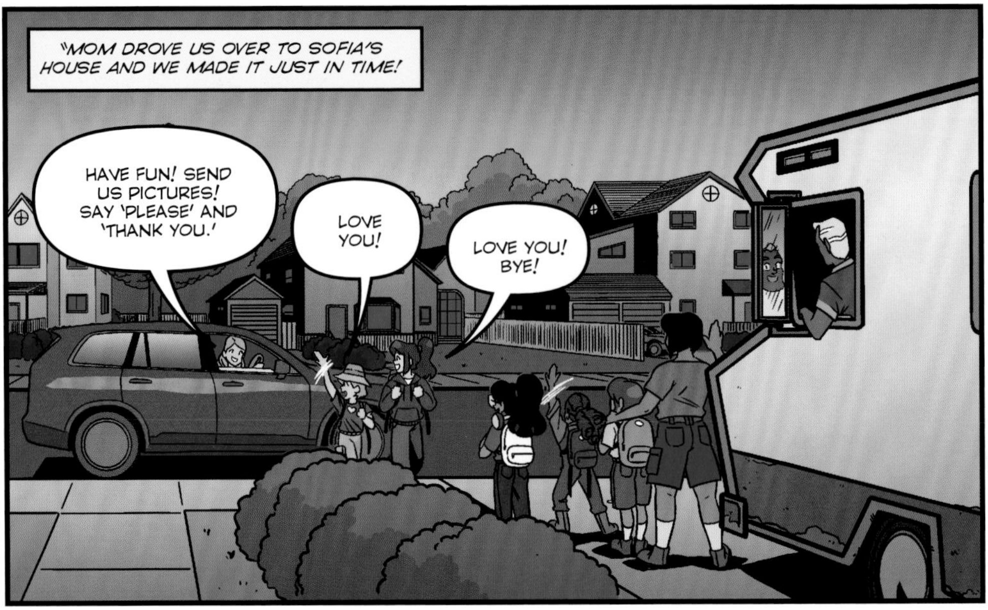
"MOM DROVE US OVER TO SOFIA'S HOUSE AND WE MADE IT JUST IN TIME!
HAVE FUN! SEND US PICTURES! SAY 'PLEASE' AND 'THANK YOU.'
LOVE YOU!
LOVE YOU! BYE!

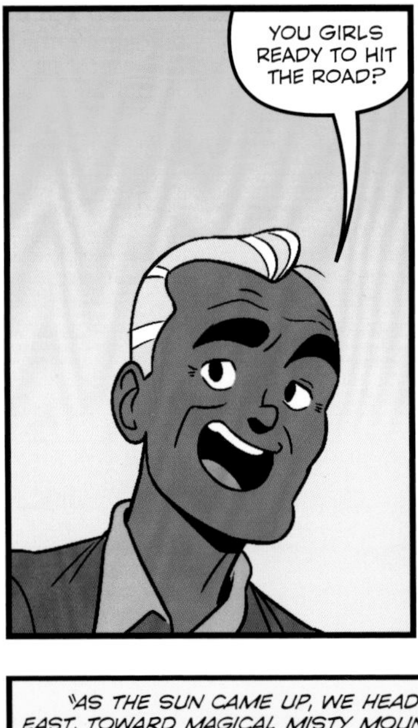
YOU GIRLS READY TO HIT THE ROAD?

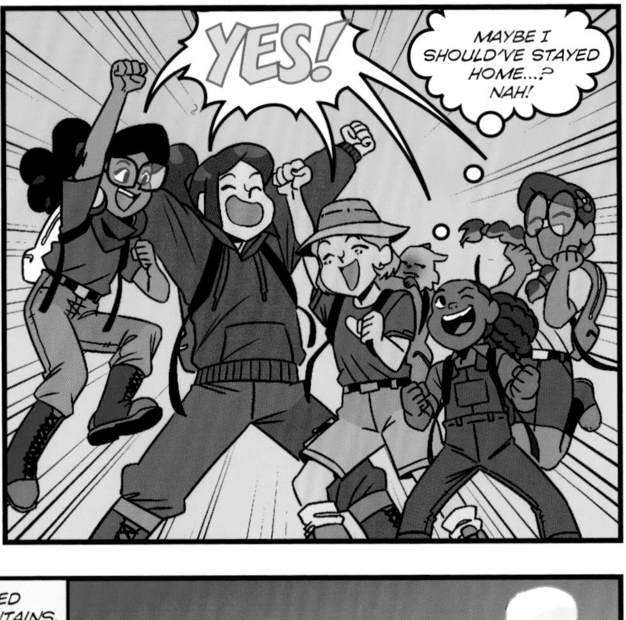
YES!
MAYBE I SHOULD'VE STAYED HOME...? NAH!

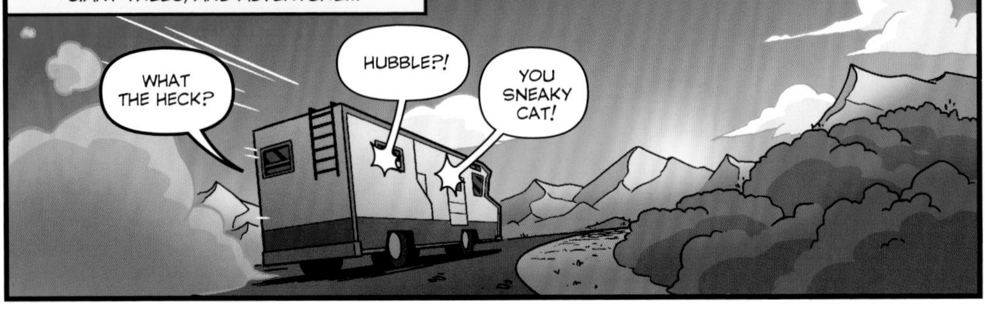
"AS THE SUN CAME UP, WE HEADED EAST, TOWARD MAGICAL MISTY MOUNTAINS, GIANT TREES, AND ADVENTURE...
WHAT THE HECK?
HUBBLE?!
YOU SNEAKY CAT!

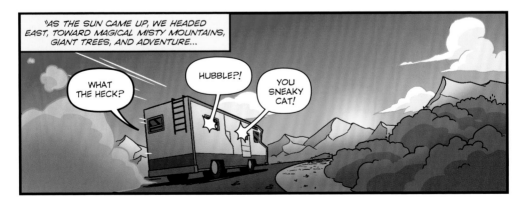

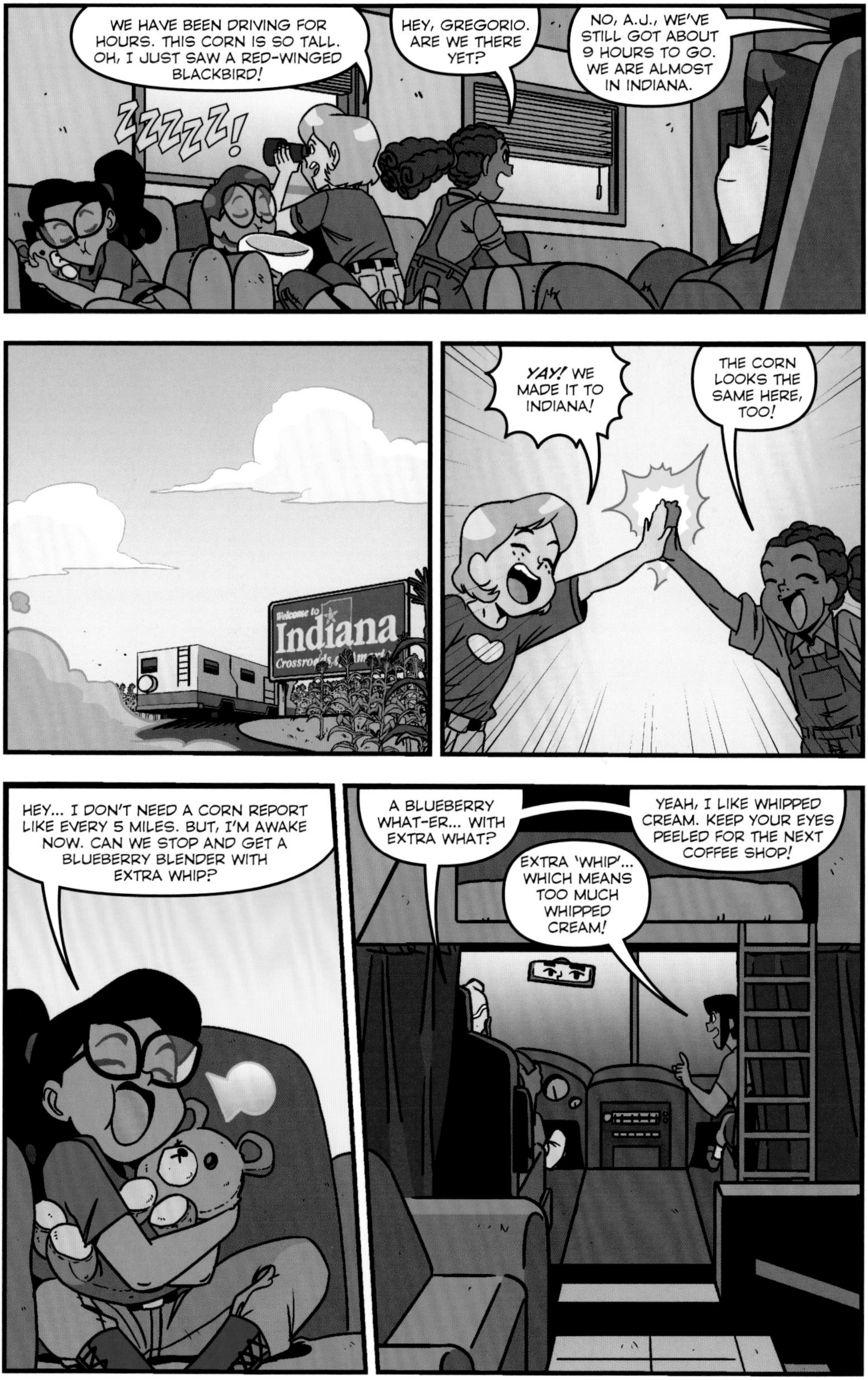

WE HAVE BEEN DRIVING FOR HOURS. THIS CORN IS SO TALL. OH, I JUST SAW A RED-WINGED BLACKBIRD!
ZZZZZ!
HEY, GREGORIO. ARE WE THERE YET?
NO, A.J., WE'VE STILL GOT ABOUT 9 HOURS TO GO. WE ARE ALMOST IN INDIANA.
Welcome to Indiana
YAY! WE MADE IT TO INDIANA!
THE CORN LOOKS THE SAME HERE, TOO!
HEY... I DON'T NEED A CORN REPORT LIKE EVERY 5 MILES. BUT, I'M AWAKE NOW. CAN WE STOP AND GET A BLUEBERRY BLENDER WITH EXTRA WHIP?
A BLUEBERRY WHAT-ER... WITH EXTRA WHAT?
EXTRA 'WHIP'... WHICH MEANS TOO MUCH WHIPPED CREAM!
YEAH, I LIKE WHIPPED CREAM. KEEP YOUR EYES PEELED FOR THE NEXT COFFEE SHOP!

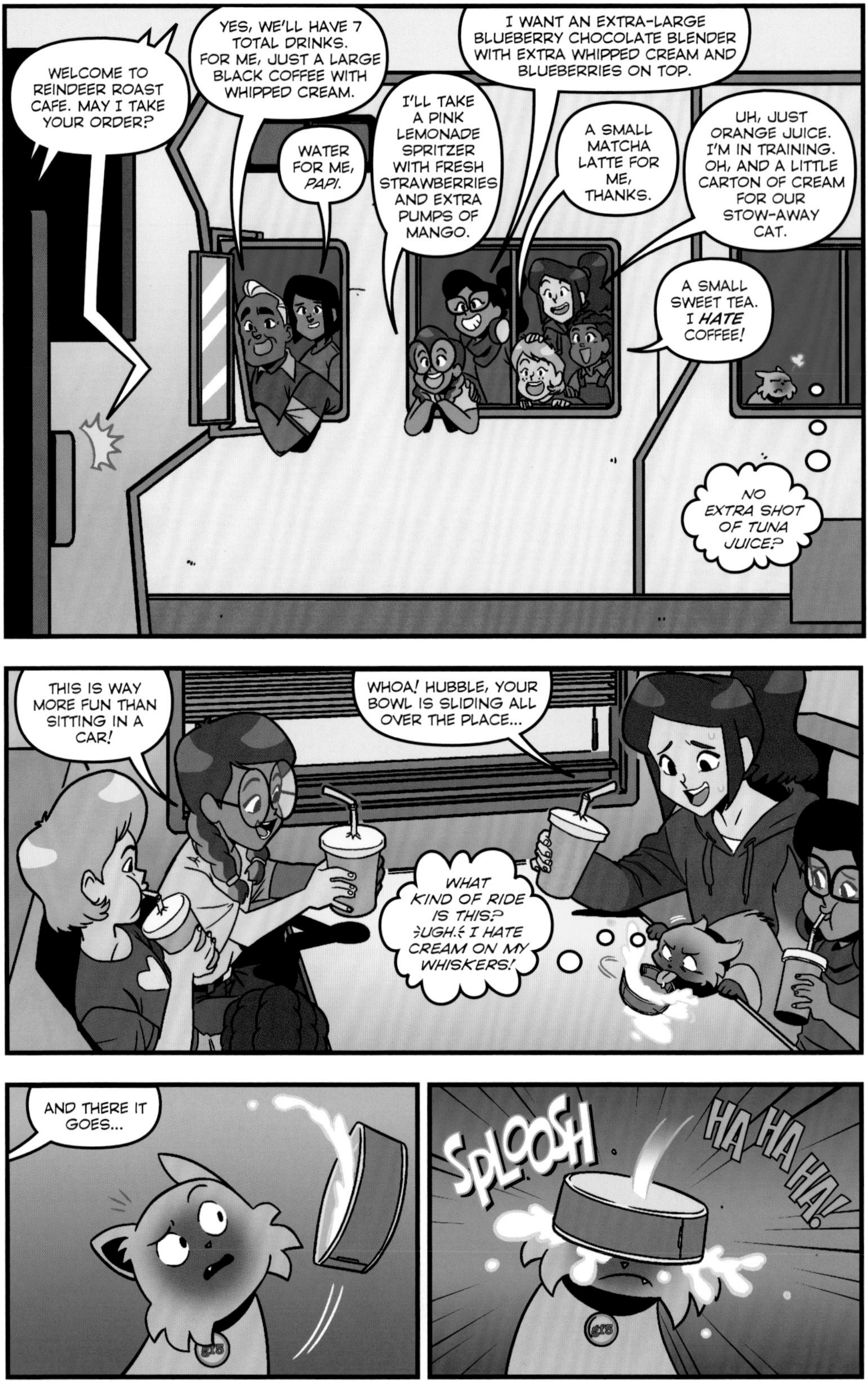
WELCOME TO REINDEER ROAST CAFE. MAY I TAKE YOUR ORDER?
YES, WE'LL HAVE 7 TOTAL DRINKS. FOR ME, JUST A LARGE BLACK COFFEE WITH WHIPPED CREAM.
WATER FOR ME, *PAPI*.
I'LL TAKE A PINK LEMONADE SPRITZER WITH FRESH STRAWBERRIES AND EXTRA PUMPS OF MANGO.
I WANT AN EXTRA-LARGE BLUEBERRY CHOCOLATE BLENDER WITH EXTRA WHIPPED CREAM AND BLUEBERRIES ON TOP.
A SMALL MATCHA LATTE FOR ME, THANKS.
UH, JUST ORANGE JUICE. I'M IN TRAINING. OH, AND A LITTLE CARTON OF CREAM FOR OUR STOW-AWAY CAT.
A SMALL SWEET TEA. I *HATE* COFFEE!
NO EXTRA SHOT OF TUNA JUICE?
THIS IS WAY MORE FUN THAN SITTING IN A CAR!
WHOA! HUBBLE, YOUR BOWL IS SLIDING ALL OVER THE PLACE...
WHAT KIND OF RIDE IS THIS? UGH. I HATE CREAM ON MY WHISKERS!
AND THERE IT GOES...
SPLOOSH
HA HA HA!

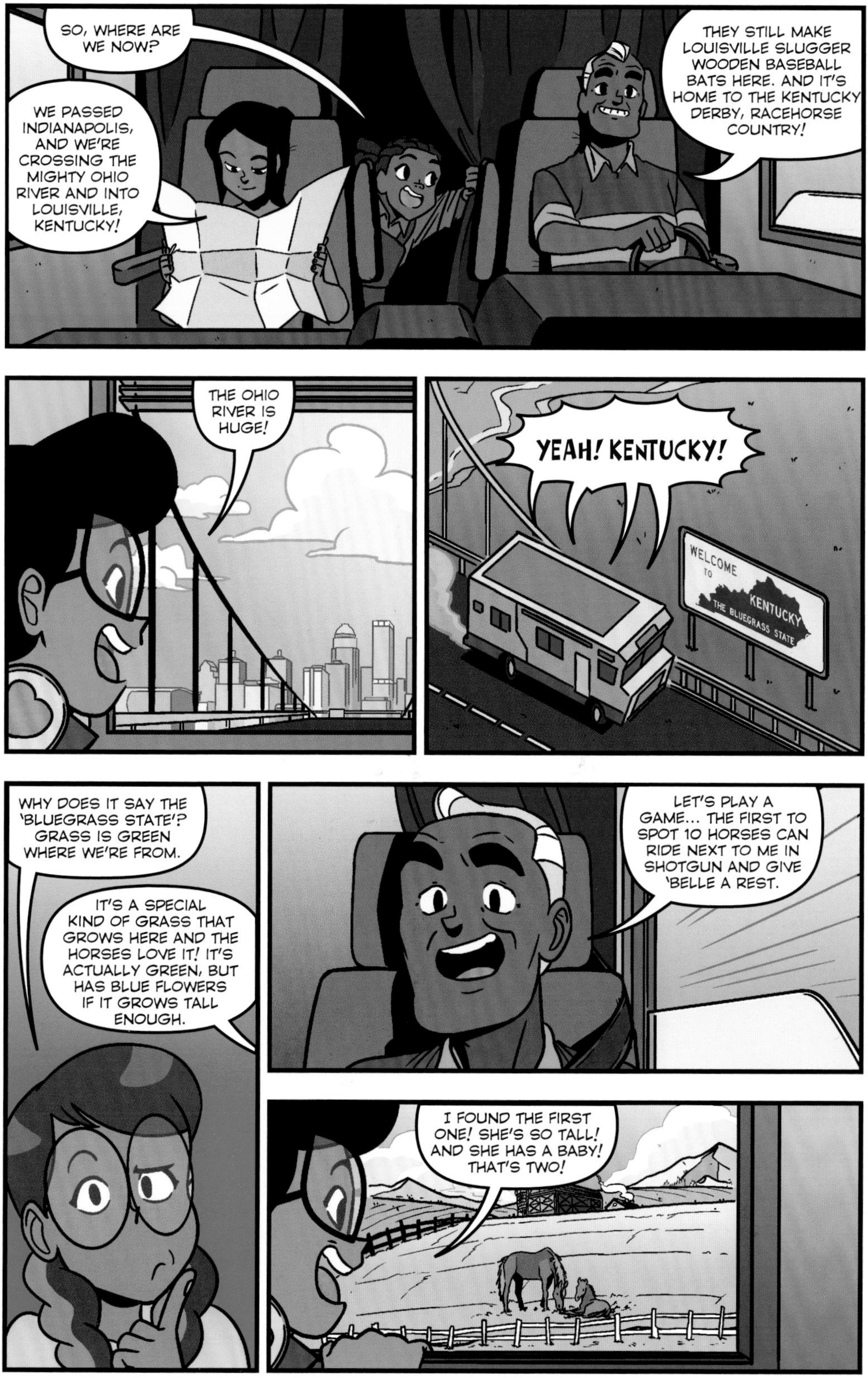
SO, WHERE ARE WE NOW?
WE PASSED INDIANAPOLIS, AND WE'RE CROSSING THE MIGHTY OHIO RIVER AND INTO LOUISVILLE, KENTUCKY!
THEY STILL MAKE LOUISVILLE SLUGGER WOODEN BASEBALL BATS HERE. AND IT'S HOME TO THE KENTUCKY DERBY, RACEHORSE COUNTRY!
THE OHIO RIVER IS HUGE!
YEAH! KENTUCKY!
WELCOME TO KENTUCKY THE BLUEGRASS STATE
WHY DOES IT SAY THE 'BLUEGRASS STATE'? GRASS IS GREEN WHERE WE'RE FROM.
IT'S A SPECIAL KIND OF GRASS THAT GROWS HERE AND THE HORSES LOVE IT! IT'S ACTUALLY GREEN, BUT HAS BLUE FLOWERS IF IT GROWS TALL ENOUGH.
LET'S PLAY A GAME... THE FIRST TO SPOT 10 HORSES CAN RIDE NEXT TO ME IN SHOTGUN AND GIVE 'BELLE A REST.
I FOUND THE FIRST ONE! SHE'S SO TALL! AND SHE HAS A BABY! THAT'S TWO!

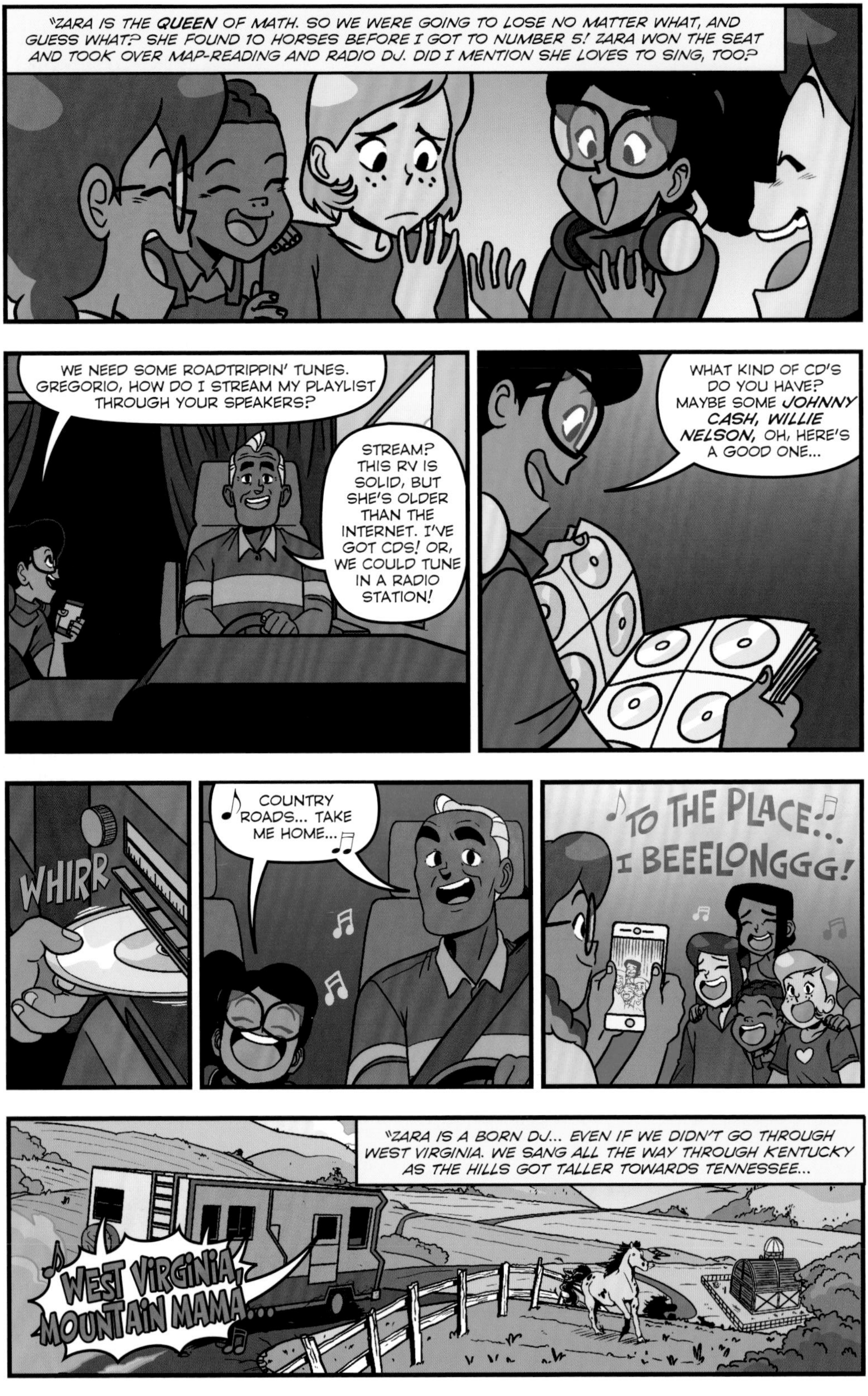
"ZARA IS THE QUEEN OF MATH. SO WE WERE GOING TO LOSE NO MATTER WHAT, AND GUESS WHAT? SHE FOUND 10 HORSES BEFORE I GOT TO NUMBER 5! ZARA WON THE SEAT AND TOOK OVER MAP-READING AND RADIO DJ. DID I MENTION SHE LOVES TO SING, TOO?
WE NEED SOME ROADTRIPPIN' TUNES. GREGORIO, HOW DO I STREAM MY PLAYLIST THROUGH YOUR SPEAKERS?
STREAM? THIS RV IS SOLID, BUT SHE'S OLDER THAN THE INTERNET. I'VE GOT CDS! OR, WE COULD TUNE IN A RADIO STATION!
WHAT KIND OF CD'S DO YOU HAVE? MAYBE SOME JOHNNY CASH, WILLIE NELSON, OH, HERE'S A GOOD ONE...
WHIRR
COUNTRY ROADS... TAKE ME HOME...
TO THE PLACE... I BEEELONGGG!
"ZARA IS A BORN DJ... EVEN IF WE DIDN'T GO THROUGH WEST VIRGINIA. WE SANG ALL THE WAY THROUGH KENTUCKY AS THE HILLS GOT TALLER TOWARDS TENNESSEE...
WEST VIRGINIA, MOUNTAIN MAMA...

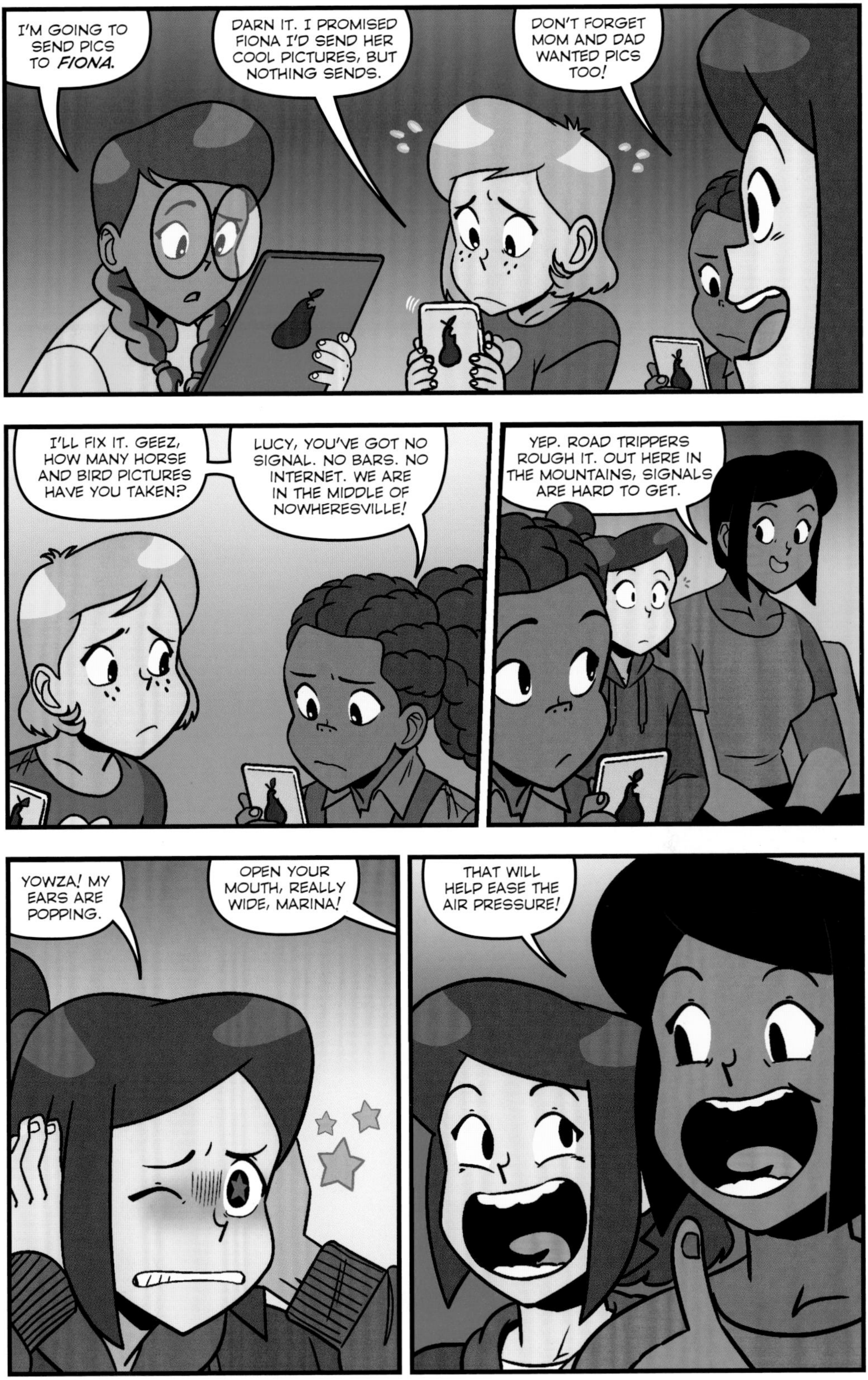
I'M GOING TO SEND PICS TO *FIONA*.
DARN IT. I PROMISED FIONA I'D SEND HER COOL PICTURES, BUT NOTHING SENDS.
DON'T FORGET MOM AND DAD WANTED PICS TOO!
I'LL FIX IT. GEEZ, HOW MANY HORSE AND BIRD PICTURES HAVE YOU TAKEN?
LUCY, YOU'VE GOT NO SIGNAL. NO BARS. NO INTERNET. WE ARE IN THE MIDDLE OF NOWHERESVILLE!
YEP. ROAD TRIPPERS ROUGH IT. OUT HERE IN THE MOUNTAINS, SIGNALS ARE HARD TO GET.
YOWZA! MY EARS ARE POPPING.
OPEN YOUR MOUTH, REALLY WIDE, MARINA!
THAT WILL HELP EASE THE AIR PRESSURE!

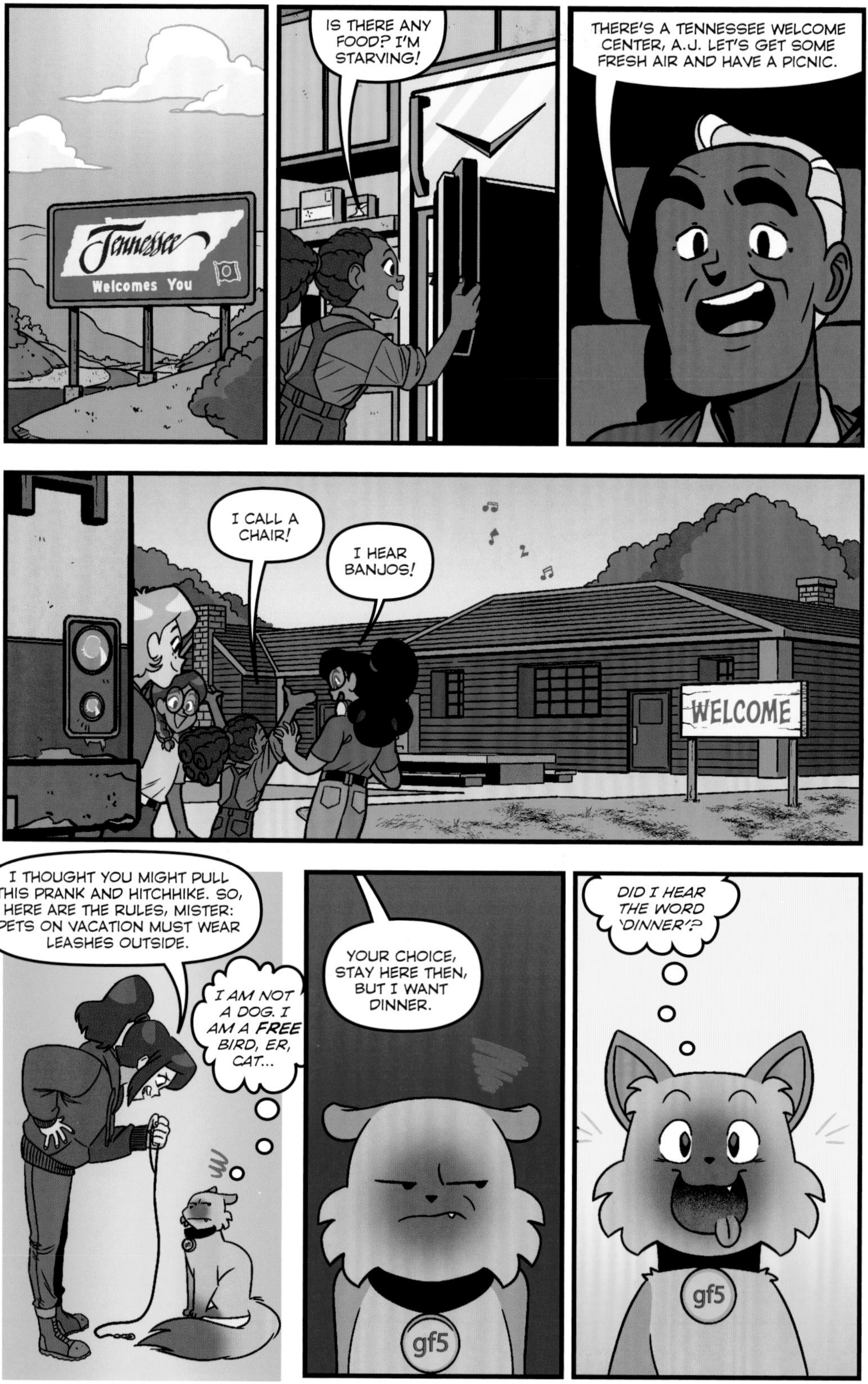
Tennessee
Welcomes You
IS THERE ANY FOOD? I'M STARVING!
THERE'S A TENNESSEE WELCOME CENTER, A.J. LET'S GET SOME FRESH AIR AND HAVE A PICNIC.
I CALL A CHAIR!
I HEAR BANJOS!
WELCOME
I THOUGHT YOU MIGHT PULL THIS PRANK AND HITCHHIKE. SO, HERE ARE THE RULES, MISTER: PETS ON VACATION MUST WEAR LEASHES OUTSIDE.
I AM NOT A DOG. I AM A FREE BIRD, ER, CAT...
YOUR CHOICE, STAY HERE THEN, BUT I WANT DINNER.
gf5
DID I HEAR THE WORD 'DINNER'?
gf5

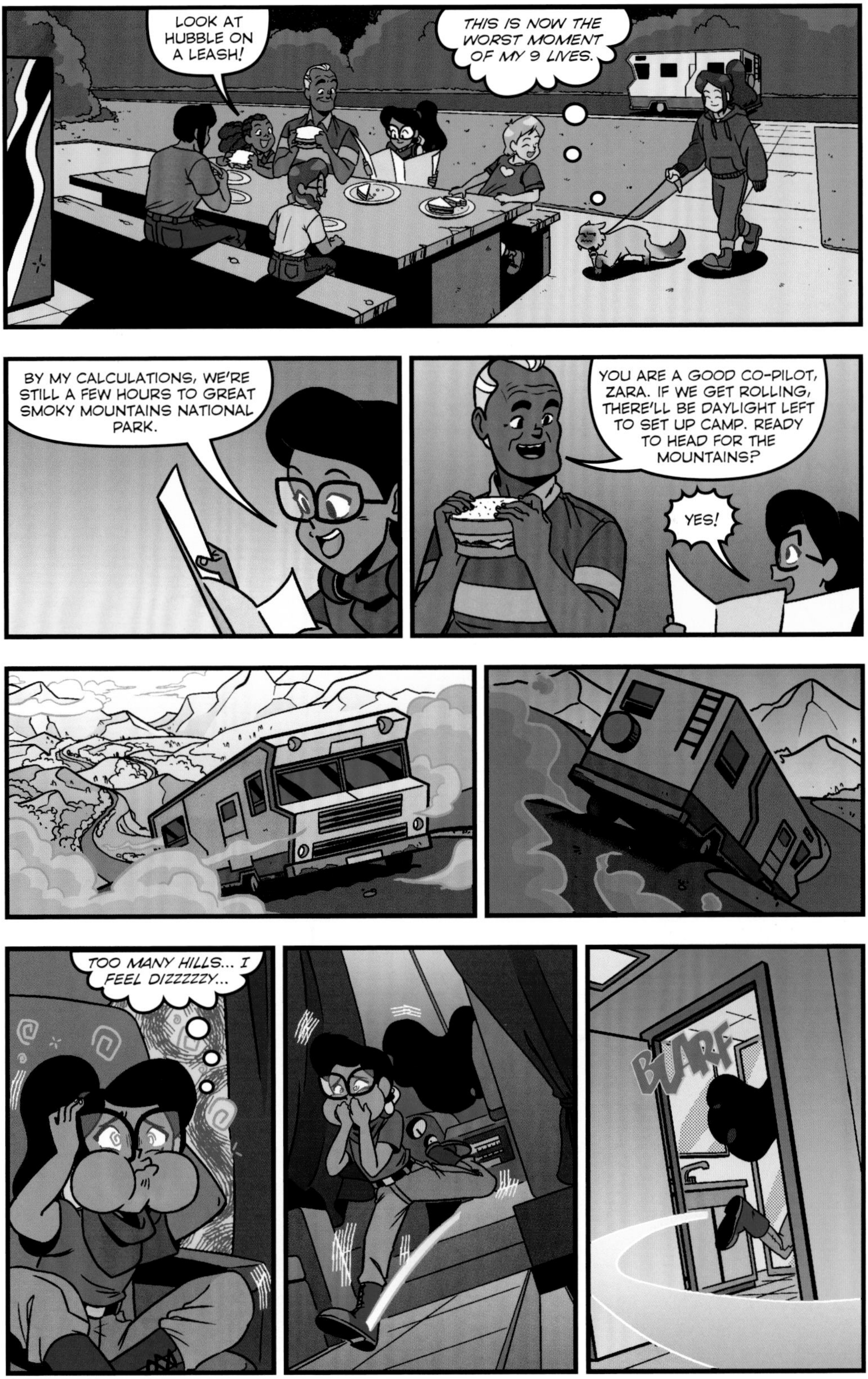
LOOK AT HUBBLE ON A LEASH!
THIS IS NOW THE WORST MOMENT OF MY 9 LIVES.
BY MY CALCULATIONS, WE'RE STILL A FEW HOURS TO GREAT SMOKY MOUNTAINS NATIONAL PARK.
YOU ARE A GOOD CO-PILOT, ZARA. IF WE GET ROLLING, THERE'LL BE DAYLIGHT LEFT TO SET UP CAMP. READY TO HEAD FOR THE MOUNTAINS?
YES!
TOO MANY HILLS... I FEEL DIZZZZZY...
BLARF

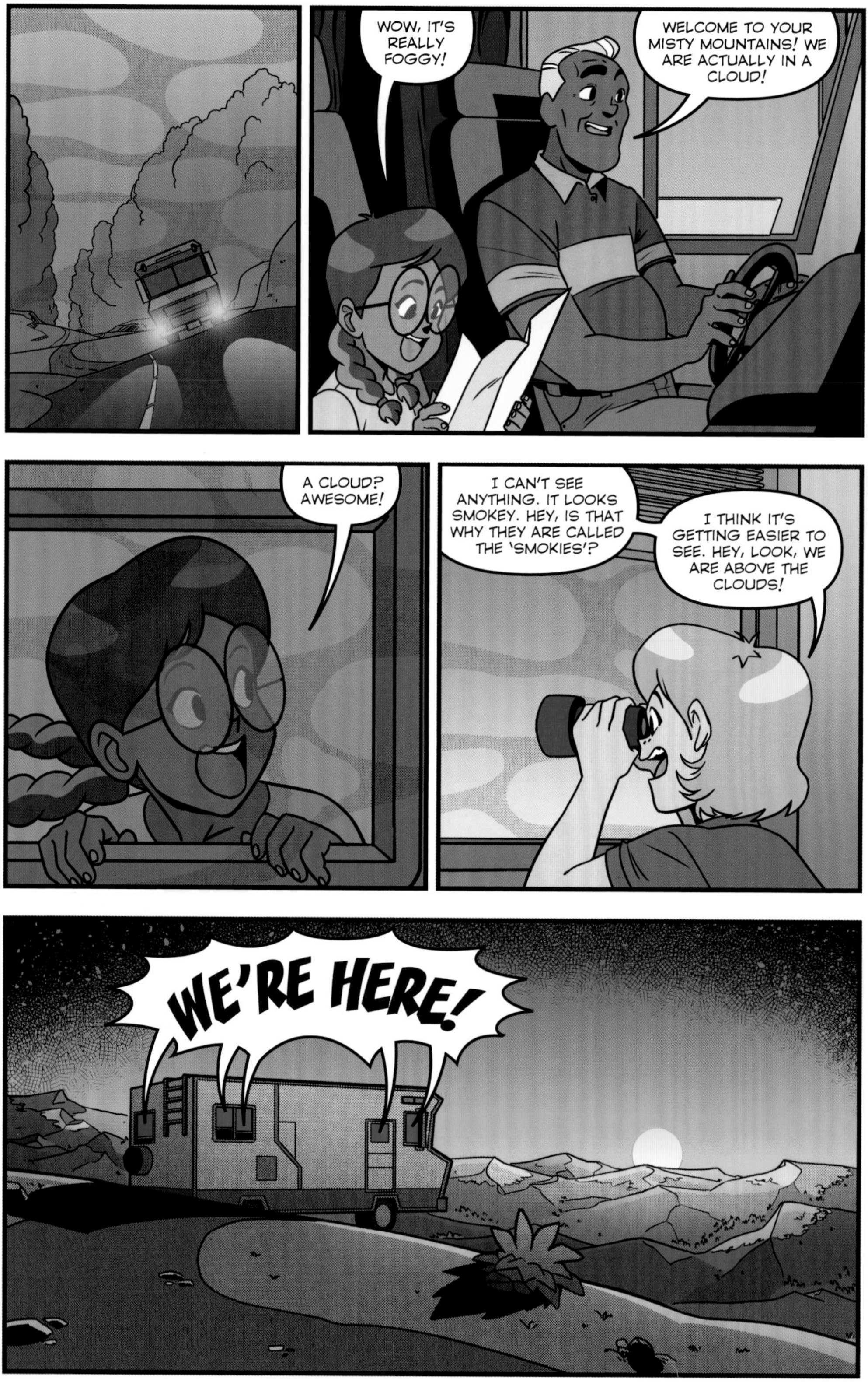
WOW, IT'S REALLY FOGGY!
WELCOME TO YOUR MISTY MOUNTAINS! WE ARE ACTUALLY IN A CLOUD!
A CLOUD? AWESOME!
I CAN'T SEE ANYTHING. IT LOOKS SMOKEY. HEY, IS THAT WHY THEY ARE CALLED THE 'SMOKIES'?
I THINK IT'S GETTING EASIER TO SEE. HEY, LOOK, WE ARE ABOVE THE CLOUDS!
WE'RE HERE!

CHAPTER FOUR: ROUGHING IT

"TWELVE HOURS LATER AND WE ARE CELEBRATING RIGHT AT THE PARK ENTRANCE. OUR ADVENTURE HAS BEGUN...

SMILE AND SAY 'SMOKIES!'

CLICK

SMOKIES!

GREAT SMOKY MOUNTAINS PARK

GOOD JOB, *PAPI*. YOU GOT US HERE SAFE AND SOUND.

AH, HEAR THE SOUND OF THE CRICKETS? ALSO, OUR OWN SET OF CRICKETS CHATTERING IN THE TENT...

WHAT COULD THOSE GIRLS POSSIBLY BE TALKING ABOUT?

CHIRP

CHIRP

THIS IS COOL. LIKE A SLUMBER PARTY FOR A WHOLE WEEK!

GOOD JOB, GIRLS. NOW, FOR THE RULES: ONE: DON'T WANDER OFF ALONE. USE THE BUDDY SYSTEM.

TWO: NO FOOD ALLOWED. A.J., THAT GOES FOR YOUR SECRET TAFFY STASH. BEARS AND RACCOONS LIKE HUMAN FOOD AND IT'S BAD FOR THEM.

AND THREE: TENT ZIPPER STAYS ZIPPED. OR WE BECOME MOSQUITO SNACKS TONIGHT, GOT IT?

AND WE WOULDN'T WANT ANY *SNAKES*, SNUGGLED ON YOUR PILLOW! RIGHT, MARINA?

THERE AREN'T ANY SNAKES HERE.

ACTUALLY, THERE IS A POISONOUS SNAKE CALLED A 'COPPERHEAD.' THEY EAT MICE AND RODENTS.

THEY ARE SHY AND DON'T BITE UNLESS YOU SCARE THEM.

GULP!

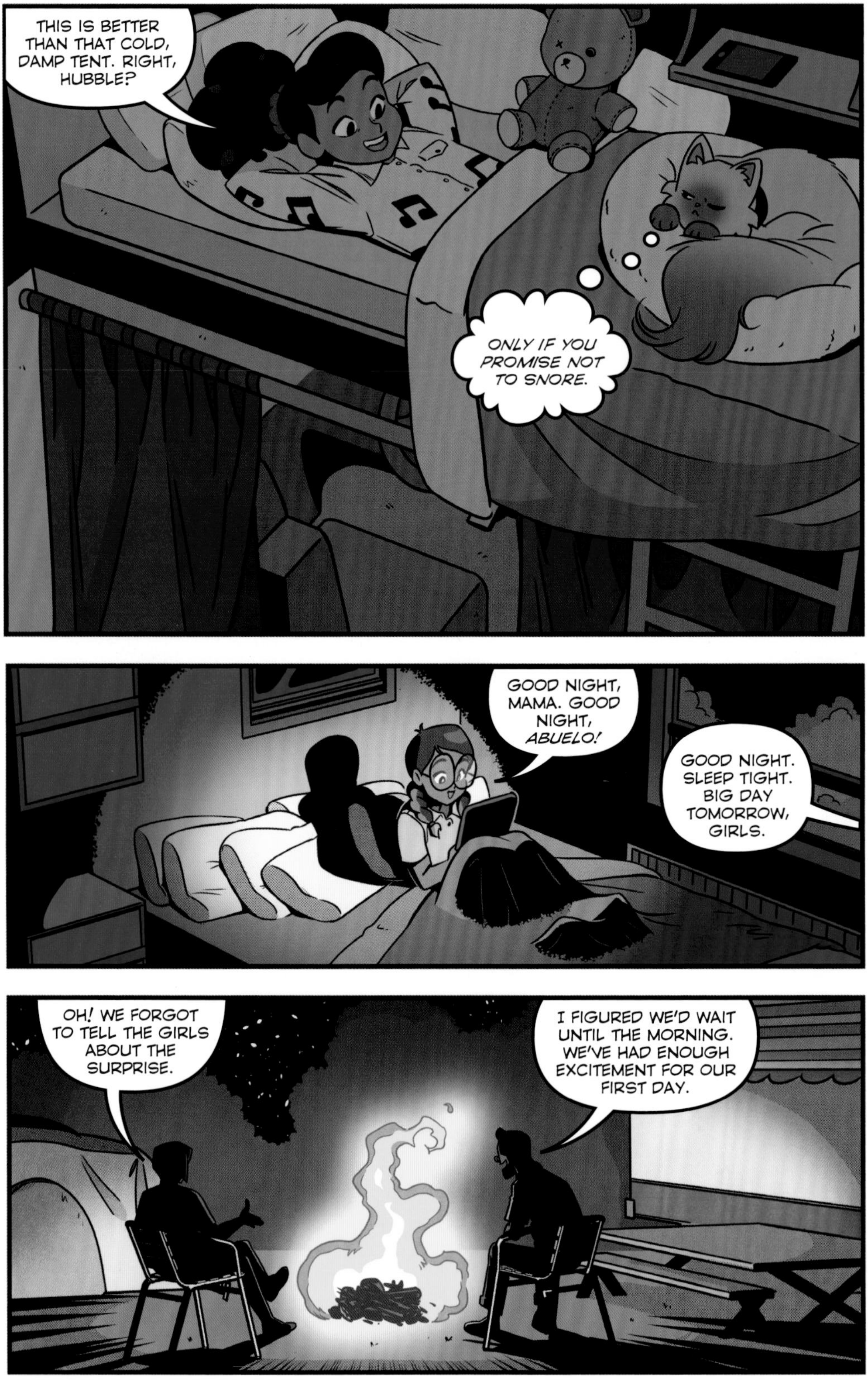
THIS IS BETTER THAN THAT COLD, DAMP TENT. RIGHT, HUBBLE?
ONLY IF YOU PROMISE NOT TO SNORE.
GOOD NIGHT, MAMA. GOOD NIGHT, ABUELO!
GOOD NIGHT. SLEEP TIGHT. BIG DAY TOMORROW, GIRLS.
OH! WE FORGOT TO TELL THE GIRLS ABOUT THE SURPRISE.
I FIGURED WE'D WAIT UNTIL THE MORNING. WE'VE HAD ENOUGH EXCITEMENT FOR OUR FIRST DAY.

"IT'S PRE-DAWN AND I HEAR THE STRANGEST THING...

≋MEWWW.≋
≋MEWW.≋

HUBBLE. GO AWAY. IT'S NOT BREAKFAST TIME.

≋MEWWW.≋
≋MEWW.≋

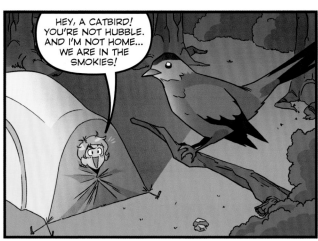

HEY, A CATBIRD! YOU'RE NOT HUBBLE. AND I'M NOT HOME... WE ARE IN THE SMOKIES!

≋MEWWW.≋
≋MEWW.≋

≋MEWW≋
≋TWEET≋
≋CHIRP≋
≋CHIRP≋
≋TWEET≋
≋CAW≋
≋CAW≋
≋TWEET≋

HELLO, MISTY MOUNTAINS.

WOW, I CAN HEAR ABOUT A HUNDRED DIFFERENT BIRDS SINGING...

IT'S CALLED THE 'DAWN CHORUS.'

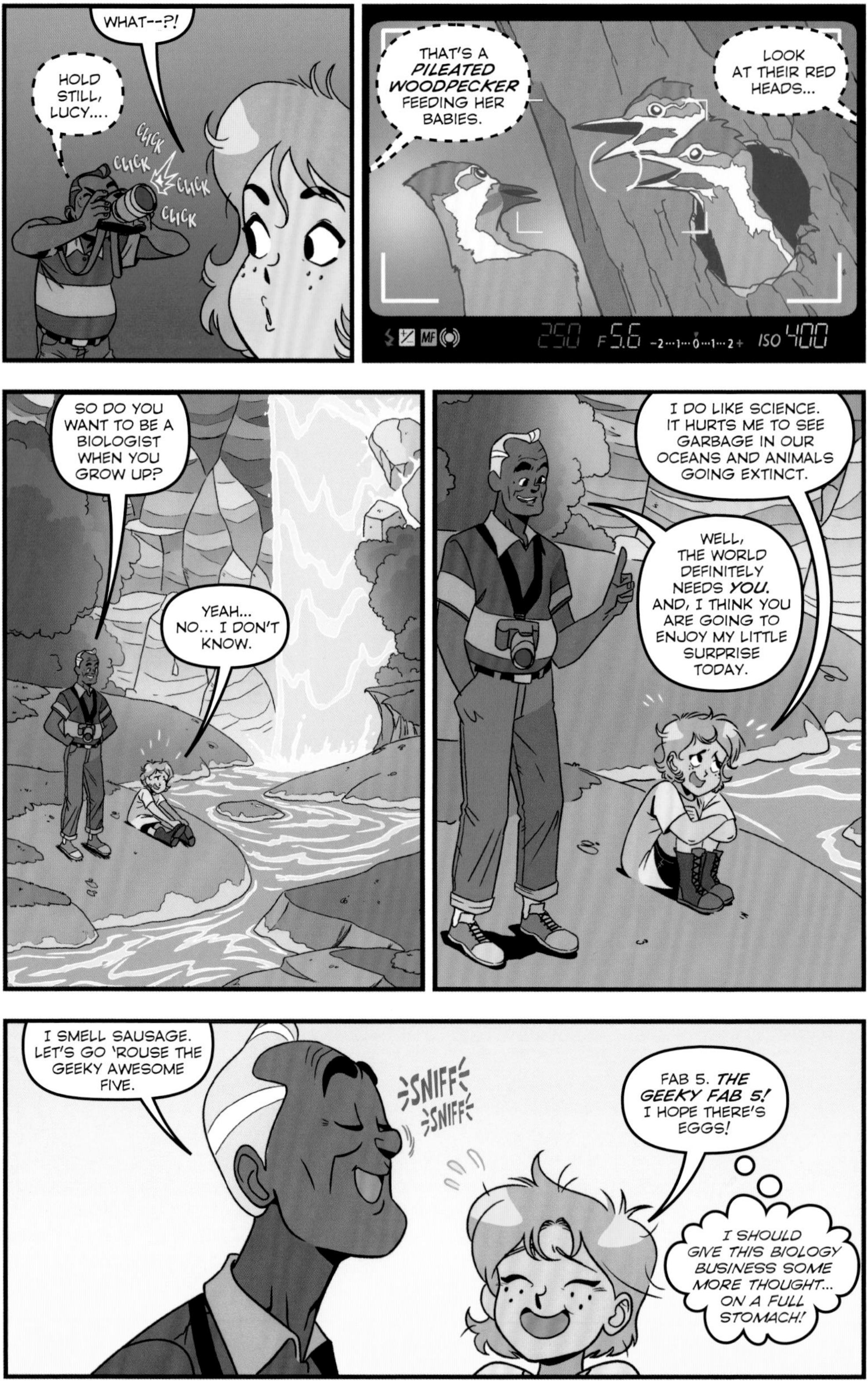
WHAT--?!
HOLD STILL, LUCY....
CLICK CLICK CLICK CLICK
THAT'S A PILEATED WOODPECKER FEEDING HER BABIES.
LOOK AT THEIR RED HEADS...
250 F5.6 -2···1···0···1···2+ ISO 400
SO DO YOU WANT TO BE A BIOLOGIST WHEN YOU GROW UP?
YEAH... NO... I DON'T KNOW.
I DO LIKE SCIENCE. IT HURTS ME TO SEE GARBAGE IN OUR OCEANS AND ANIMALS GOING EXTINCT.
WELL, THE WORLD DEFINITELY NEEDS YOU. AND, I THINK YOU ARE GOING TO ENJOY MY LITTLE SURPRISE TODAY.
I SMELL SAUSAGE. LET'S GO 'ROUSE THE GEEKY AWESOME FIVE.
SNIFF SNIFF
FAB 5. THE GEEKY FAB 5! I HOPE THERE'S EGGS!
I SHOULD GIVE THIS BIOLOGY BUSINESS SOME MORE THOUGHT... ON A FULL STOMACH!

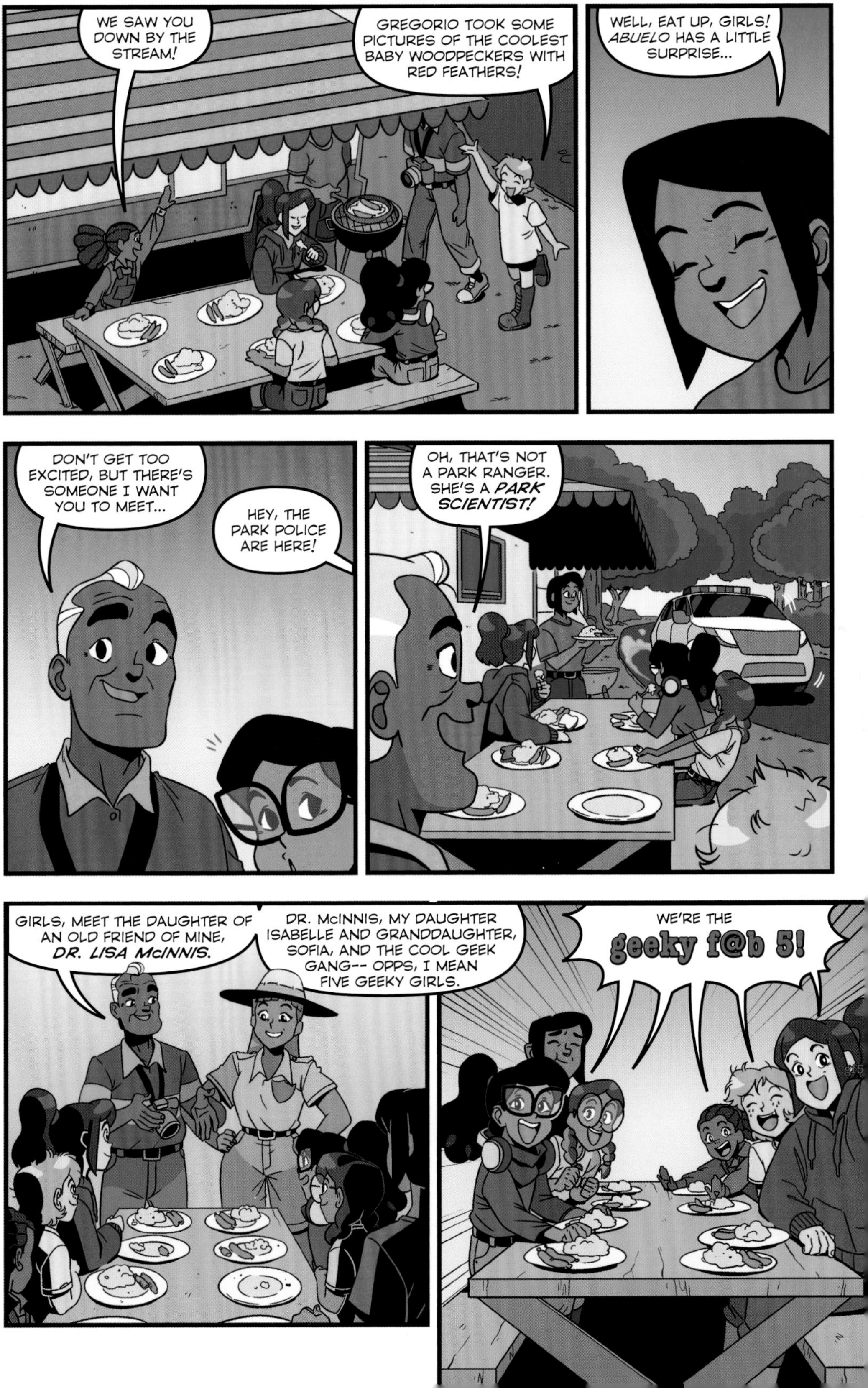
WE SAW YOU DOWN BY THE STREAM!
GREGORIO TOOK SOME PICTURES OF THE COOLEST BABY WOODPECKERS WITH RED FEATHERS!
WELL, EAT UP, GIRLS! *ABUELO* HAS A LITTLE SURPRISE...
DON'T GET TOO EXCITED, BUT THERE'S SOMEONE I WANT YOU TO MEET...
HEY, THE PARK POLICE ARE HERE!
OH, THAT'S NOT A PARK RANGER. SHE'S A ***PARK SCIENTIST!***
GIRLS, MEET THE DAUGHTER OF AN OLD FRIEND OF MINE, ***DR. LISA McINNIS***.
DR. McINNIS, MY DAUGHTER ISABELLE AND GRANDDAUGHTER, SOFIA, AND THE COOL GEEK GANG-- OPPS, I MEAN FIVE GEEKY GIRLS.
WE'RE THE geeky f@b 5!

CHAPTER FIVE: SMOKY SCIENCE SQUAD

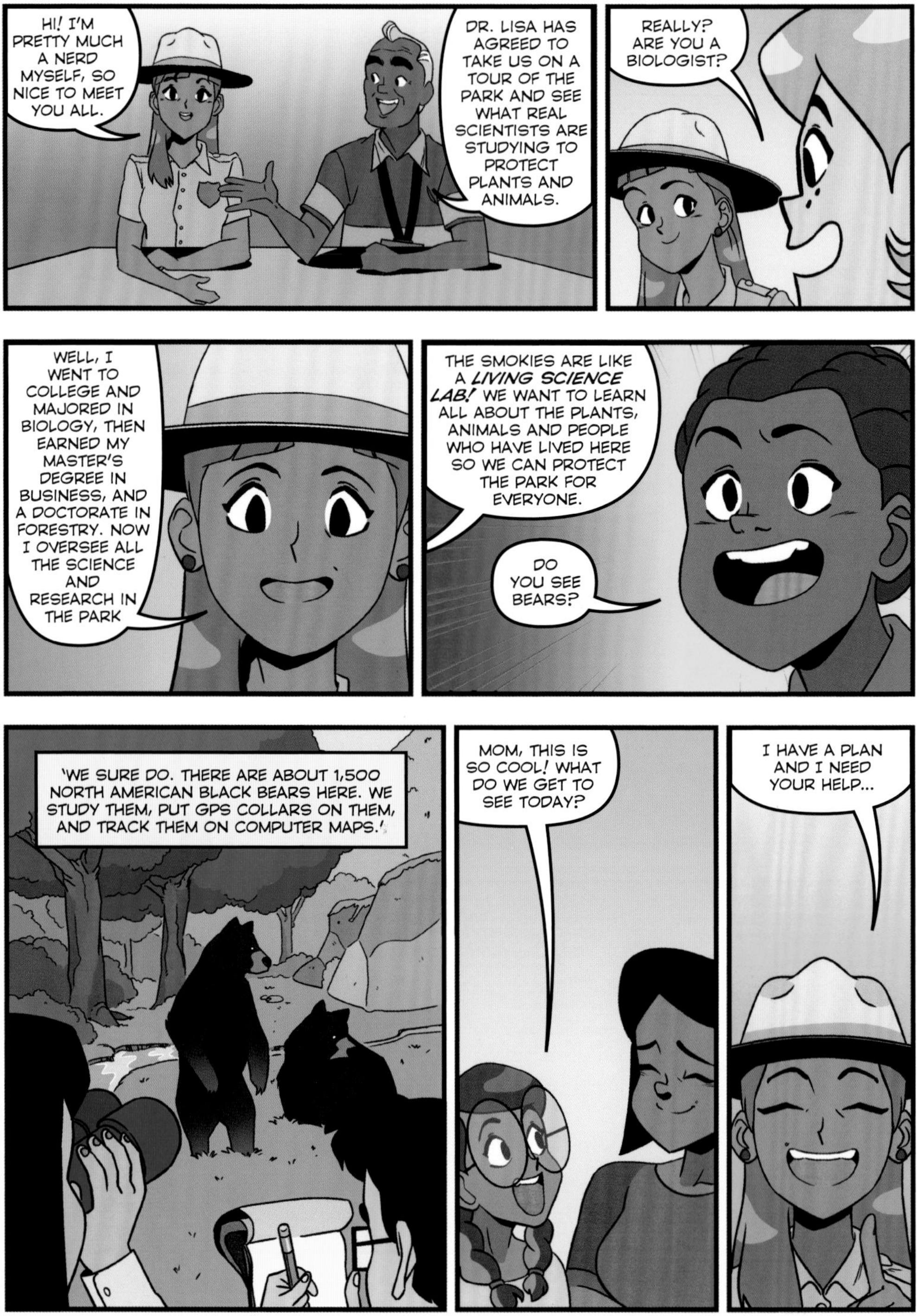
HI! I'M PRETTY MUCH A NERD MYSELF, SO NICE TO MEET YOU ALL.
DR. LISA HAS AGREED TO TAKE US ON A TOUR OF THE PARK AND SEE WHAT REAL SCIENTISTS ARE STUDYING TO PROTECT PLANTS AND ANIMALS.
REALLY? ARE YOU A BIOLOGIST?
WELL, I WENT TO COLLEGE AND MAJORED IN BIOLOGY, THEN EARNED MY MASTER'S DEGREE IN BUSINESS, AND A DOCTORATE IN FORESTRY. NOW I OVERSEE ALL THE SCIENCE AND RESEARCH IN THE PARK
THE SMOKIES ARE LIKE A *LIVING SCIENCE LAB!* WE WANT TO LEARN ALL ABOUT THE PLANTS, ANIMALS AND PEOPLE WHO HAVE LIVED HERE SO WE CAN PROTECT THE PARK FOR EVERYONE.
DO YOU SEE BEARS?
'WE SURE DO. THERE ARE ABOUT 1,500 NORTH AMERICAN BLACK BEARS HERE. WE STUDY THEM, PUT GPS COLLARS ON THEM, AND TRACK THEM ON COMPUTER MAPS.'
MOM, THIS IS SO COOL! WHAT DO WE GET TO SEE TODAY?
I HAVE A PLAN AND I NEED YOUR HELP...

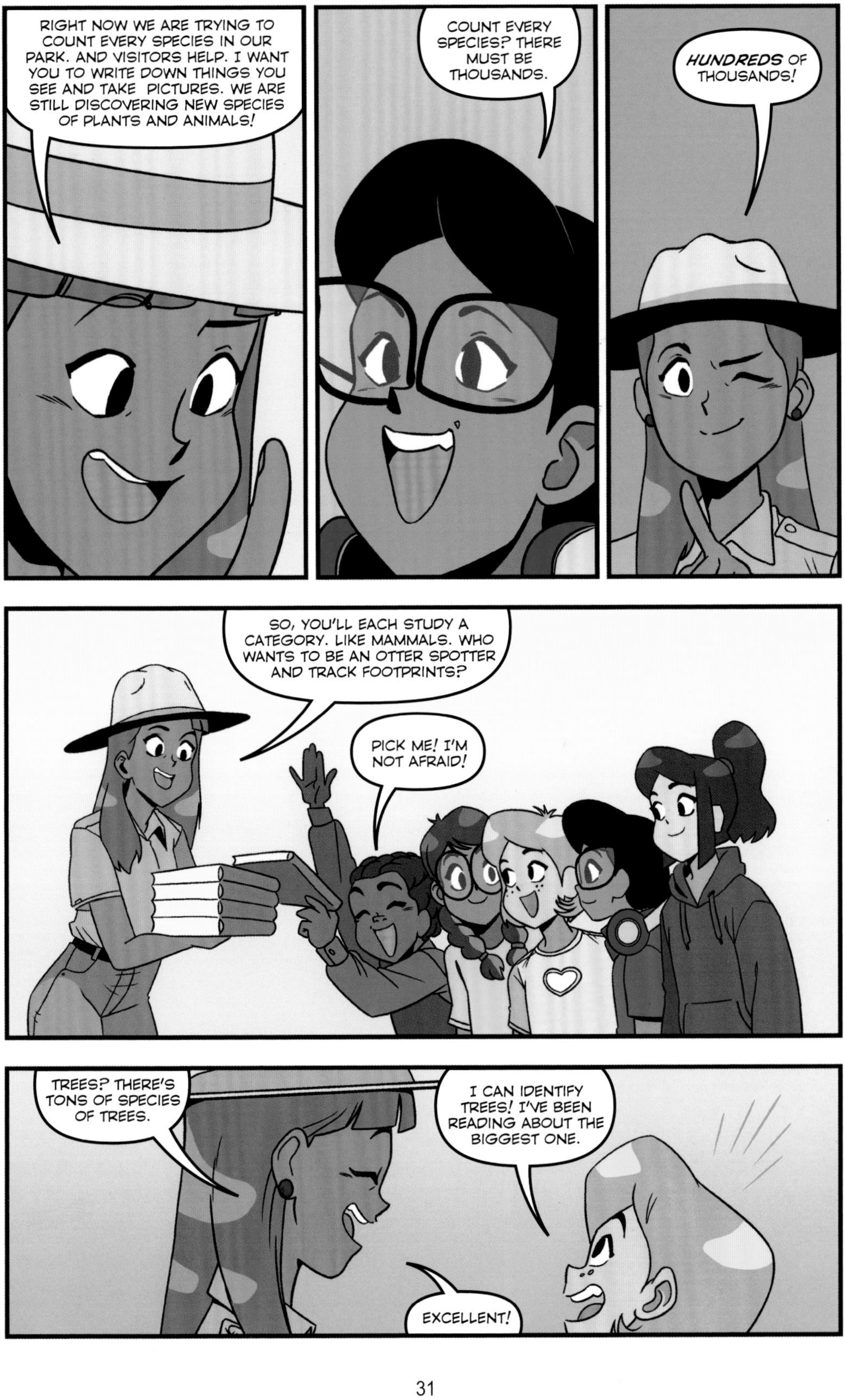
RIGHT NOW WE ARE TRYING TO COUNT EVERY SPECIES IN OUR PARK. AND VISITORS HELP. I WANT YOU TO WRITE DOWN THINGS YOU SEE AND TAKE PICTURES. WE ARE STILL DISCOVERING NEW SPECIES OF PLANTS AND ANIMALS!
COUNT EVERY SPECIES? THERE MUST BE THOUSANDS.
HUNDREDS OF THOUSANDS!
SO, YOU'LL EACH STUDY A CATEGORY. LIKE MAMMALS. WHO WANTS TO BE AN OTTER SPOTTER AND TRACK FOOTPRINTS?
PICK ME! I'M NOT AFRAID!
TREES? THERE'S TONS OF SPECIES OF TREES.
I CAN IDENTIFY TREES! I'VE BEEN READING ABOUT THE BIGGEST ONE.
EXCELLENT!

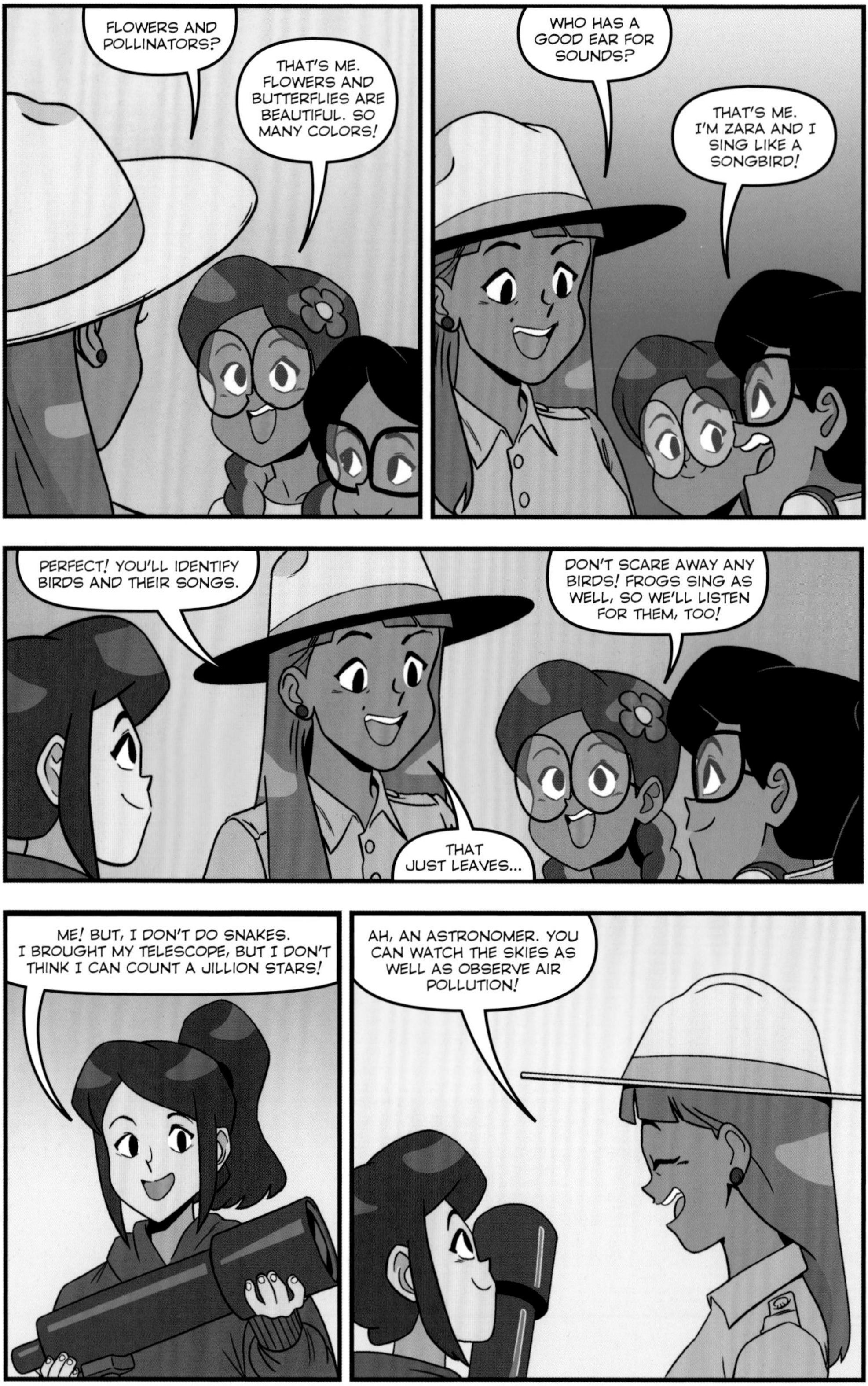
FLOWERS AND POLLINATORS?
THAT'S ME. FLOWERS AND BUTTERFLIES ARE BEAUTIFUL. SO MANY COLORS!
WHO HAS A GOOD EAR FOR SOUNDS?
THAT'S ME. I'M ZARA AND I SING LIKE A SONGBIRD!
PERFECT! YOU'LL IDENTIFY BIRDS AND THEIR SONGS.
DON'T SCARE AWAY ANY BIRDS! FROGS SING AS WELL, SO WE'LL LISTEN FOR THEM, TOO!
THAT JUST LEAVES...
ME! BUT, I DON'T DO SNAKES. I BROUGHT MY TELESCOPE, BUT I DON'T THINK I CAN COUNT A JILLION STARS!
AH, AN ASTRONOMER. YOU CAN WATCH THE SKIES AS WELL AS OBSERVE AIR POLLUTION!

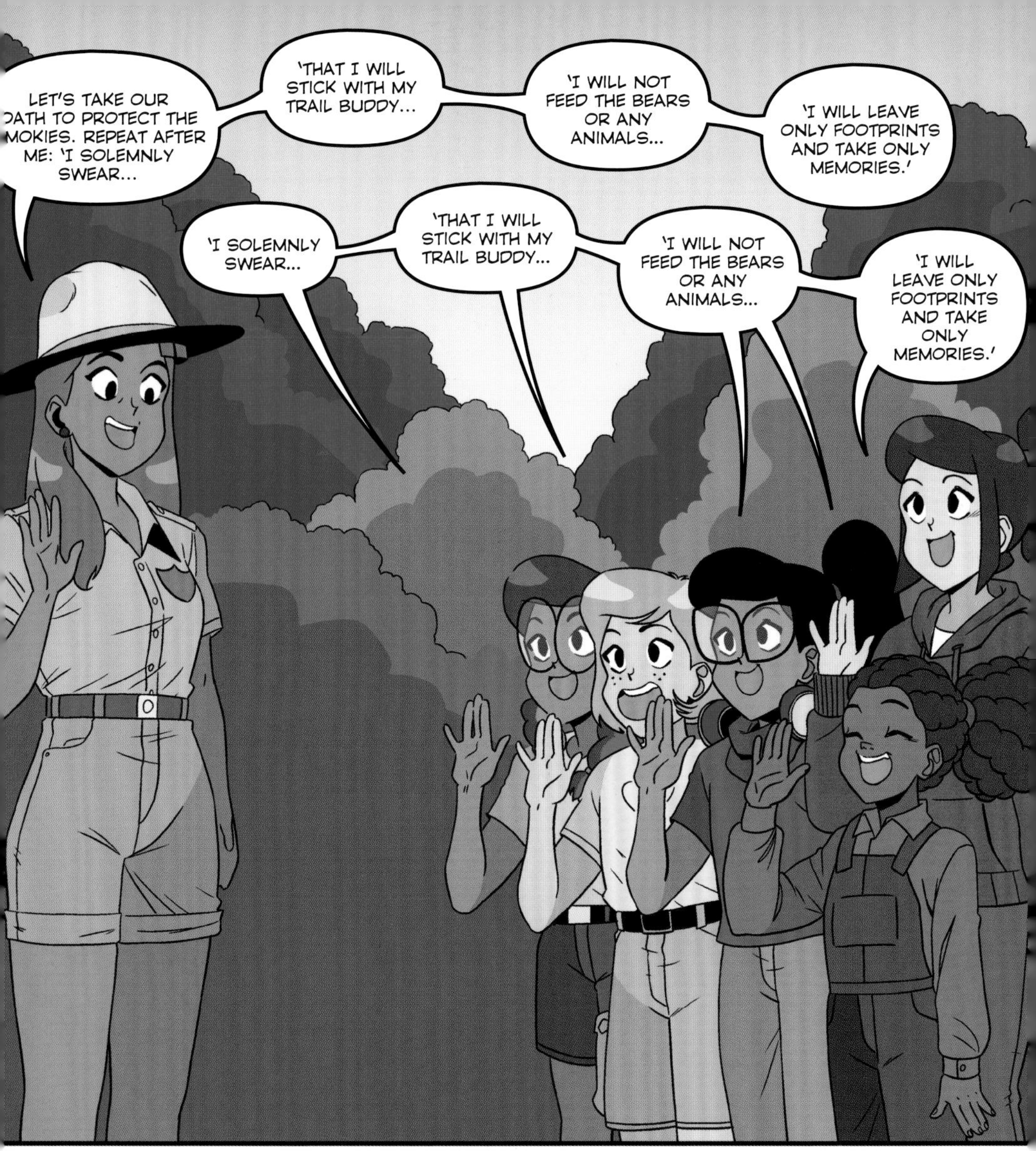
LET'S TAKE OUR OATH TO PROTECT THE SMOKIES. REPEAT AFTER ME: 'I SOLEMNLY SWEAR...
'THAT I WILL STICK WITH MY TRAIL BUDDY...
'I WILL NOT FEED THE BEARS OR ANY ANIMALS...
'I WILL LEAVE ONLY FOOTPRINTS AND TAKE ONLY MEMORIES.'
'I SOLEMNLY SWEAR...
'THAT I WILL STICK WITH MY TRAIL BUDDY...
'I WILL NOT FEED THE BEARS OR ANY ANIMALS...
'I WILL LEAVE ONLY FOOTPRINTS AND TAKE ONLY MEMORIES.'

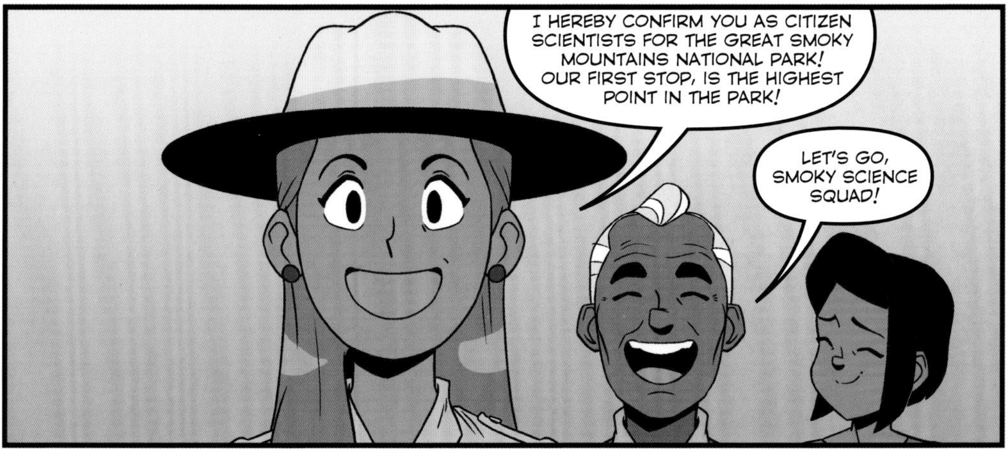
I HEREBY CONFIRM YOU AS CITIZEN SCIENTISTS FOR THE GREAT SMOKY MOUNTAINS NATIONAL PARK! OUR FIRST STOP, IS THE HIGHEST POINT IN THE PARK!
LET'S GO, SMOKY SCIENCE SQUAD!

CHAPTER SIX: ON TOP OF OLD SMOKY

"THE SMOKY MOUNTAINS ARE HIGH AND THE TUNNELS ARE FUN TO DRIVE THROUGH. DR. LISA WAS TAKING US TO THE HIGHEST POINT IN TENNESSEE!

"FINALLY WE MADE IT!

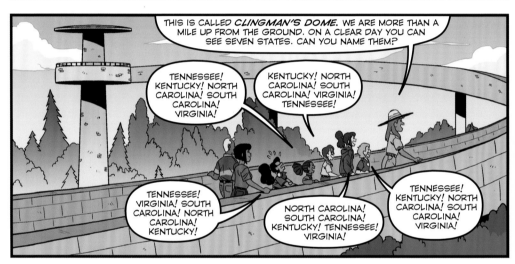

THIS IS CALLED *CLINGMAN'S DOME.* WE ARE MORE THAN A MILE UP FROM THE GROUND. ON A CLEAR DAY YOU CAN SEE SEVEN STATES. CAN YOU NAME THEM?

TENNESSEE! KENTUCKY! NORTH CAROLINA! SOUTH CAROLINA! VIRGINIA!

KENTUCKY! NORTH CAROLINA! SOUTH CAROLINA! VIRGINIA! TENNESSEE!

TENNESSEE! VIRGINIA! SOUTH CAROLINA! NORTH CAROLINA! KENTUCKY!

NORTH CAROLINA! SOUTH CAROLINA! KENTUCKY! TENNESSEE! VIRGINIA!

TENNESSEE! KENTUCKY! NORTH CAROLINA! SOUTH CAROLINA! VIRGINIA!

≶HUFF!≶ THAT'S ONLY *FIVE* STATES! ≶PUFF!≶

WHO SAID HIKING IS FUN?

WHAT ARE THE OTHER TWO STATES?

ALABAMA AND MISSISSIPPI!

OH, WE SHOULD HAVE THOUGHT OF THAT--WOW!

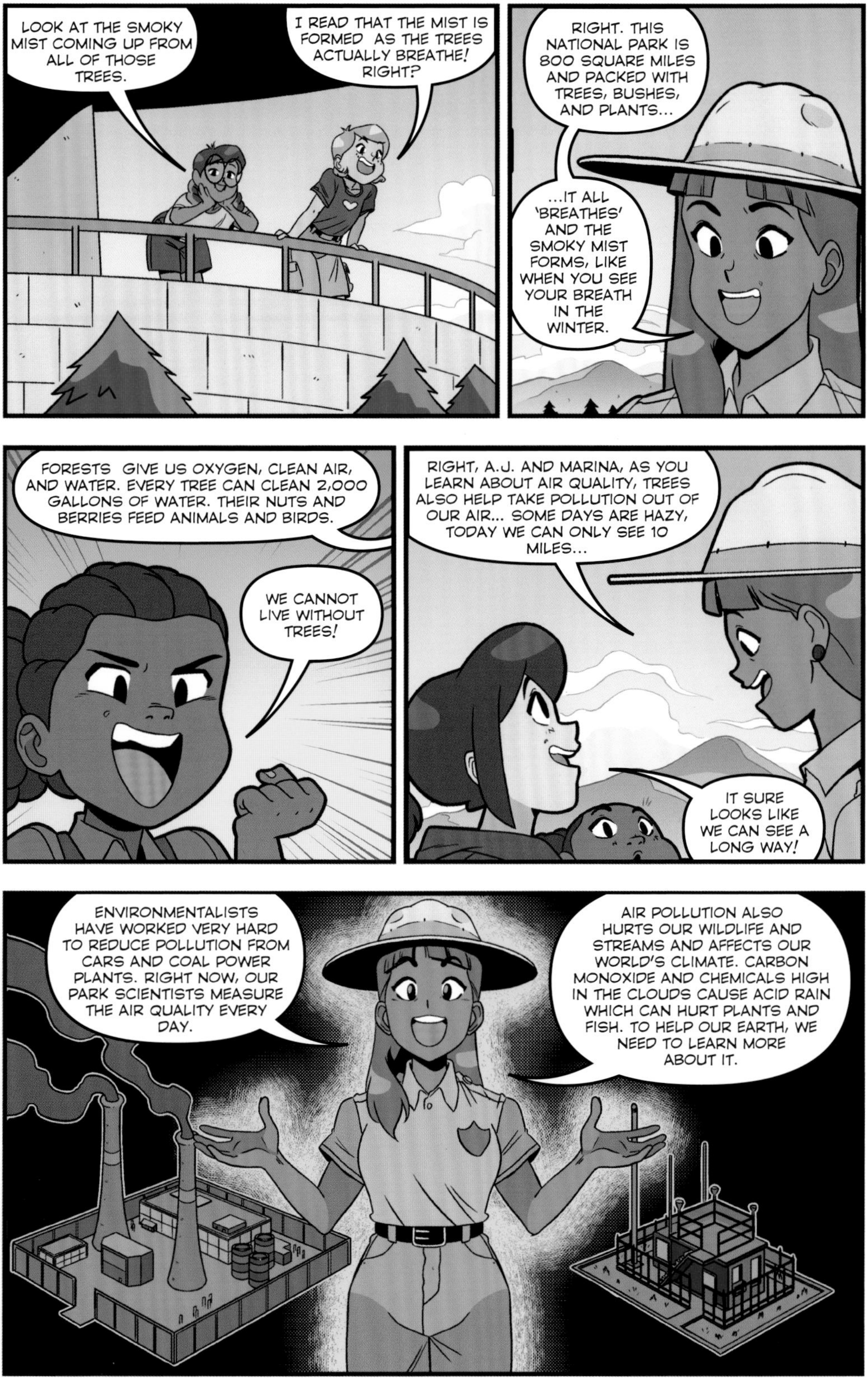
LOOK AT THE SMOKY MIST COMING UP FROM ALL OF THOSE TREES.
I READ THAT THE MIST IS FORMED AS THE TREES ACTUALLY BREATHE! RIGHT?
RIGHT. THIS NATIONAL PARK IS 800 SQUARE MILES AND PACKED WITH TREES, BUSHES, AND PLANTS...
...IT ALL 'BREATHES' AND THE SMOKY MIST FORMS, LIKE WHEN YOU SEE YOUR BREATH IN THE WINTER.
FORESTS GIVE US OXYGEN, CLEAN AIR, AND WATER. EVERY TREE CAN CLEAN 2,000 GALLONS OF WATER. THEIR NUTS AND BERRIES FEED ANIMALS AND BIRDS.
WE CANNOT LIVE WITHOUT TREES!
RIGHT, A.J. AND MARINA, AS YOU LEARN ABOUT AIR QUALITY, TREES ALSO HELP TAKE POLLUTION OUT OF OUR AIR... SOME DAYS ARE HAZY, TODAY WE CAN ONLY SEE 10 MILES...
IT SURE LOOKS LIKE WE CAN SEE A LONG WAY!
ENVIRONMENTALISTS HAVE WORKED VERY HARD TO REDUCE POLLUTION FROM CARS AND COAL POWER PLANTS. RIGHT NOW, OUR PARK SCIENTISTS MEASURE THE AIR QUALITY EVERY DAY.
AIR POLLUTION ALSO HURTS OUR WILDLIFE AND STREAMS AND AFFECTS OUR WORLD'S CLIMATE. CARBON MONOXIDE AND CHEMICALS HIGH IN THE CLOUDS CAUSE ACID RAIN WHICH CAN HURT PLANTS AND FISH. TO HELP OUR EARTH, WE NEED TO LEARN MORE ABOUT IT.

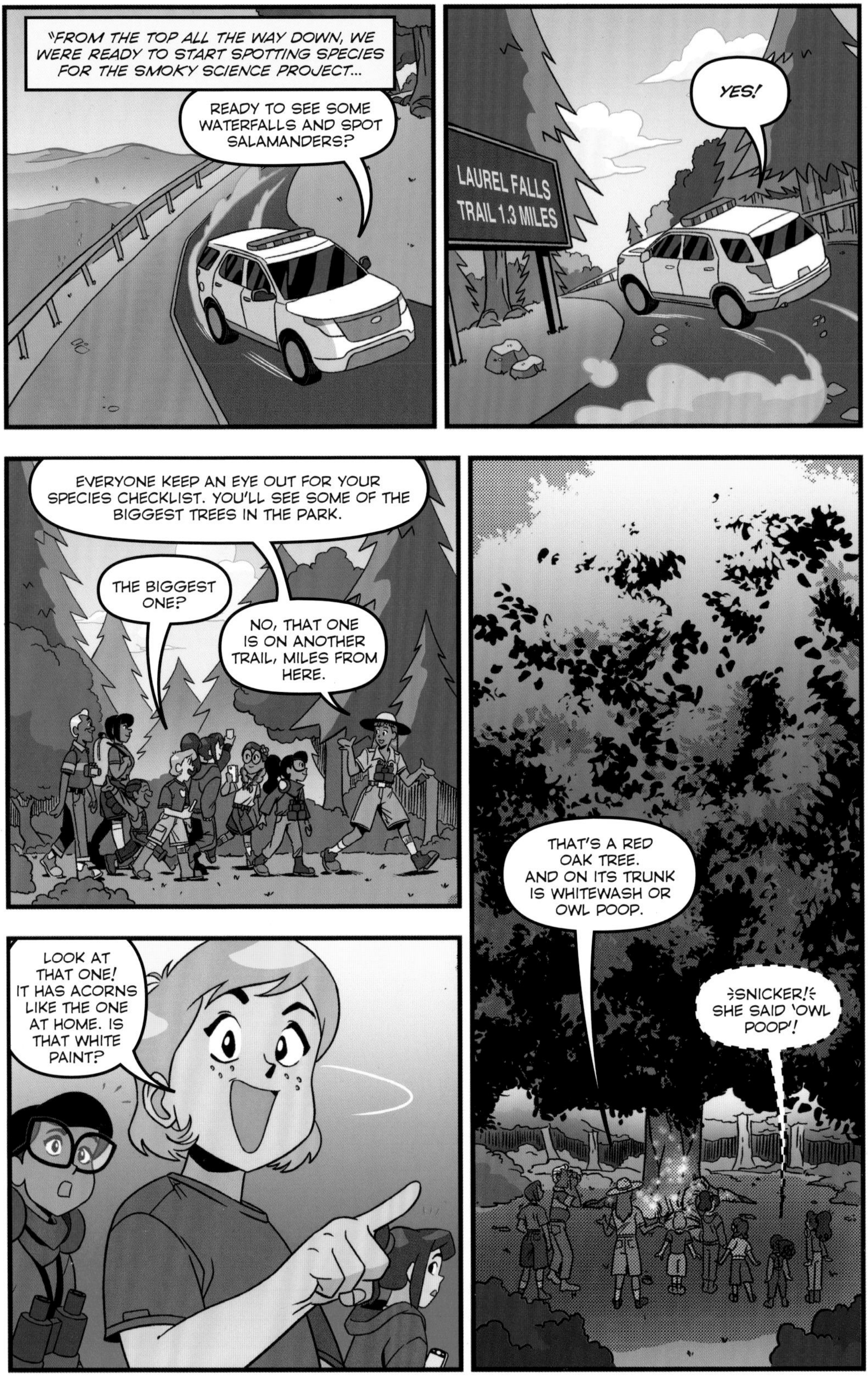
"FROM THE TOP ALL THE WAY DOWN, WE WERE READY TO START SPOTTING SPECIES FOR THE SMOKY SCIENCE PROJECT...
READY TO SEE SOME WATERFALLS AND SPOT SALAMANDERS?
LAUREL FALLS TRAIL 1.3 MILES
YES!
EVERYONE KEEP AN EYE OUT FOR YOUR SPECIES CHECKLIST. YOU'LL SEE SOME OF THE BIGGEST TREES IN THE PARK.
THE BIGGEST ONE?
NO, THAT ONE IS ON ANOTHER TRAIL, MILES FROM HERE.
LOOK AT THAT ONE! IT HAS ACORNS LIKE THE ONE AT HOME. IS THAT WHITE PAINT?
THAT'S A RED OAK TREE. AND ON ITS TRUNK IS WHITEWASH OR OWL POOP.
SNICKER! SHE SAID 'OWL POOP'!

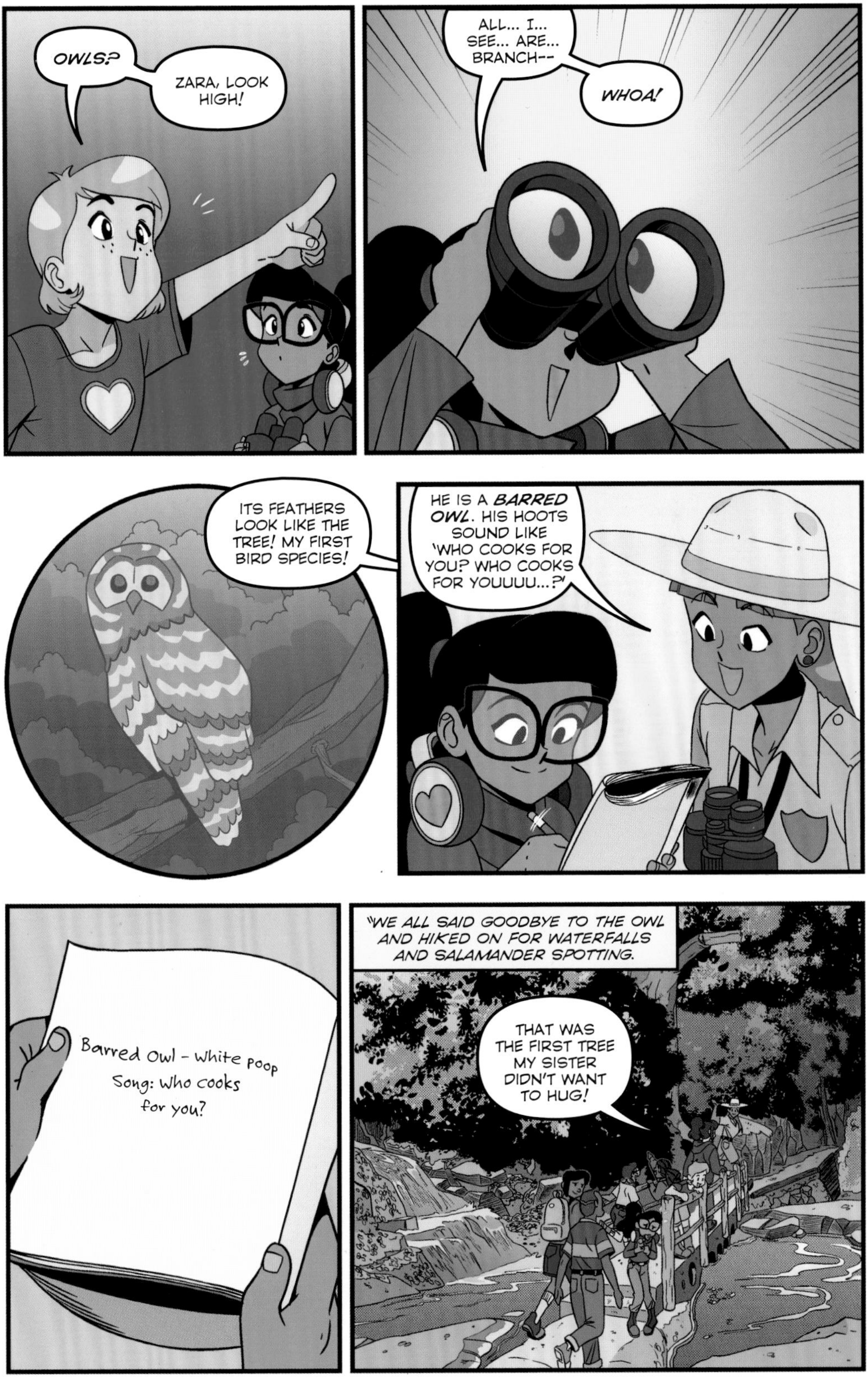
OWLS?
ZARA, LOOK HIGH!
ALL... I... SEE... ARE... BRANCH--
WHOA!
ITS FEATHERS LOOK LIKE THE TREE! MY FIRST BIRD SPECIES!
HE IS A BARRED OWL. HIS HOOTS SOUND LIKE 'WHO COOKS FOR YOU? WHO COOKS FOR YOUUUU...?'
Barred Owl - White poop
Song: Who cooks for you?
"WE ALL SAID GOODBYE TO THE OWL AND HIKED ON FOR WATERFALLS AND SALAMANDER SPOTTING.
THAT WAS THE FIRST TREE MY SISTER DIDN'T WANT TO HUG!

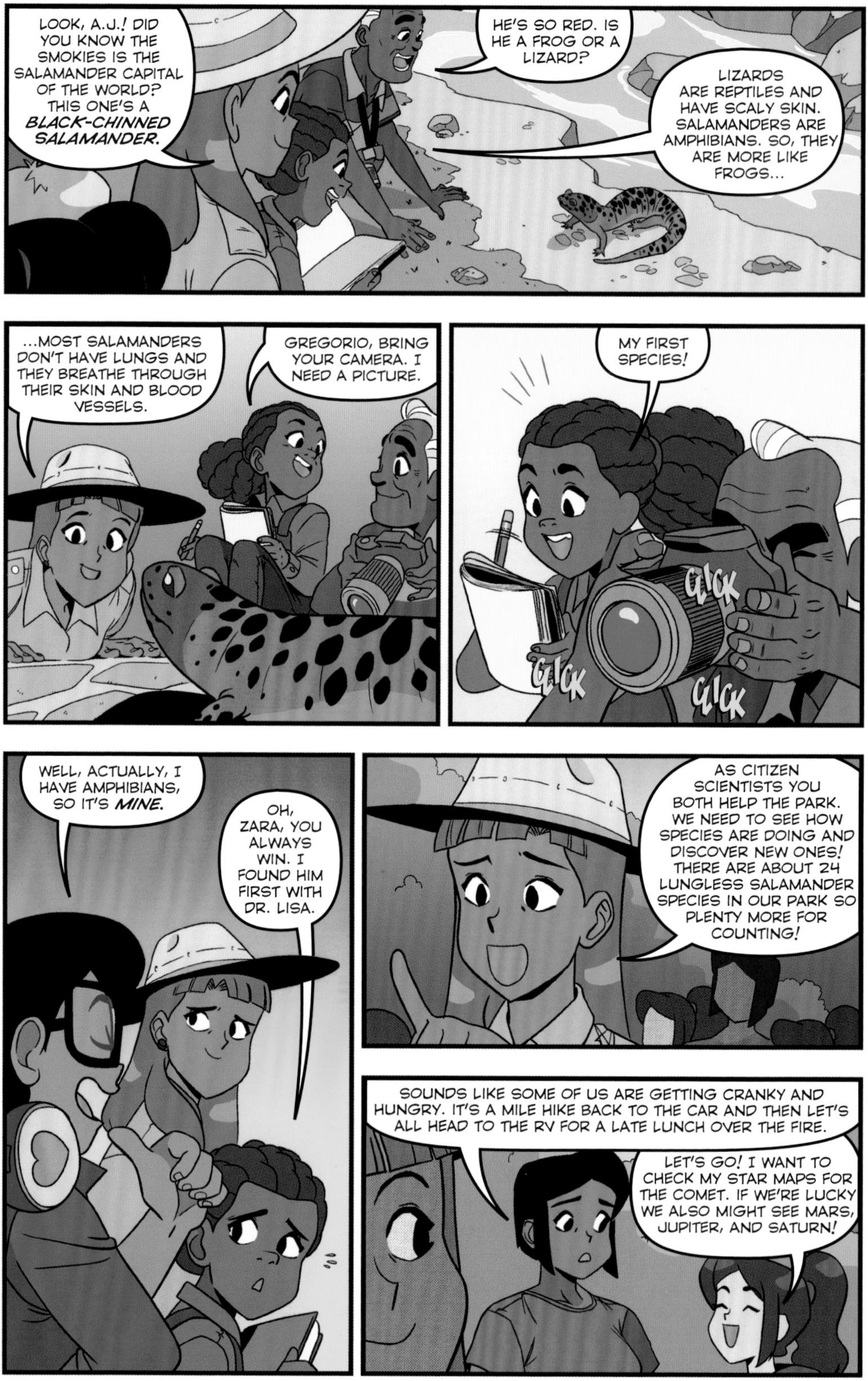
LOOK, A.J.! DID YOU KNOW THE SMOKIES IS THE SALAMANDER CAPITAL OF THE WORLD? THIS ONE'S A *BLACK-CHINNED SALAMANDER.*
HE'S SO RED. IS HE A FROG OR A LIZARD?
LIZARDS ARE REPTILES AND HAVE SCALY SKIN. SALAMANDERS ARE AMPHIBIANS. SO, THEY ARE MORE LIKE FROGS...
...MOST SALAMANDERS DON'T HAVE LUNGS AND THEY BREATHE THROUGH THEIR SKIN AND BLOOD VESSELS.
GREGORIO, BRING YOUR CAMERA. I NEED A PICTURE.
MY FIRST SPECIES!
CLICK
CLICK
CLICK
WELL, ACTUALLY, I HAVE AMPHIBIANS, SO IT'S ***MINE.***
OH, ZARA, YOU ALWAYS WIN. I FOUND HIM FIRST WITH DR. LISA.
AS CITIZEN SCIENTISTS YOU BOTH HELP THE PARK. WE NEED TO SEE HOW SPECIES ARE DOING AND DISCOVER NEW ONES! THERE ARE ABOUT 24 LUNGLESS SALAMANDER SPECIES IN OUR PARK SO PLENTY MORE FOR COUNTING!
SOUNDS LIKE SOME OF US ARE GETTING CRANKY AND HUNGRY. IT'S A MILE HIKE BACK TO THE CAR AND THEN LET'S ALL HEAD TO THE RV FOR A LATE LUNCH OVER THE FIRE.
LET'S GO! I WANT TO CHECK MY STAR MAPS FOR THE COMET. IF WE'RE LUCKY WE ALSO MIGHT SEE MARS, JUPITER, AND SATURN!

CHAPTER SEVEN: NATURE'S FIREWORKS

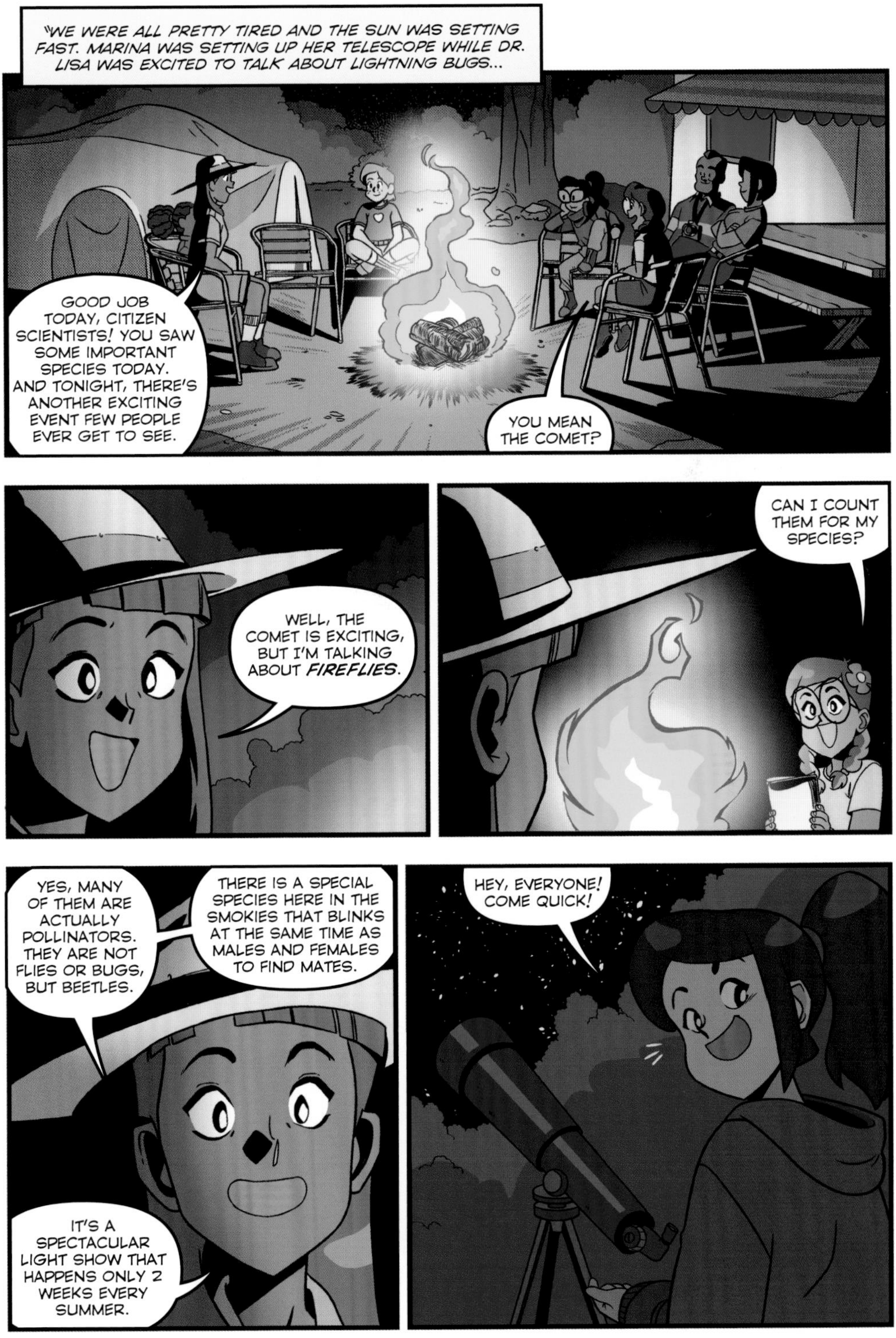

"WE WERE ALL PRETTY TIRED AND THE SUN WAS SETTING FAST. MARINA WAS SETTING UP HER TELESCOPE WHILE DR. LISA WAS EXCITED TO TALK ABOUT LIGHTNING BUGS...
GOOD JOB TODAY, CITIZEN SCIENTISTS! YOU SAW SOME IMPORTANT SPECIES TODAY. AND TONIGHT, THERE'S ANOTHER EXCITING EVENT FEW PEOPLE EVER GET TO SEE.
YOU MEAN THE COMET?
WELL, THE COMET IS EXCITING, BUT I'M TALKING ABOUT *FIREFLIES*.
CAN I COUNT THEM FOR MY SPECIES?
YES, MANY OF THEM ARE ACTUALLY POLLINATORS. THEY ARE NOT FLIES OR BUGS, BUT BEETLES.
THERE IS A SPECIAL SPECIES HERE IN THE SMOKIES THAT BLINKS AT THE SAME TIME AS MALES AND FEMALES TO FIND MATES.
IT'S A SPECTACULAR LIGHT SHOW THAT HAPPENS ONLY 2 WEEKS EVERY SUMMER.
HEY, EVERYONE! COME QUICK!

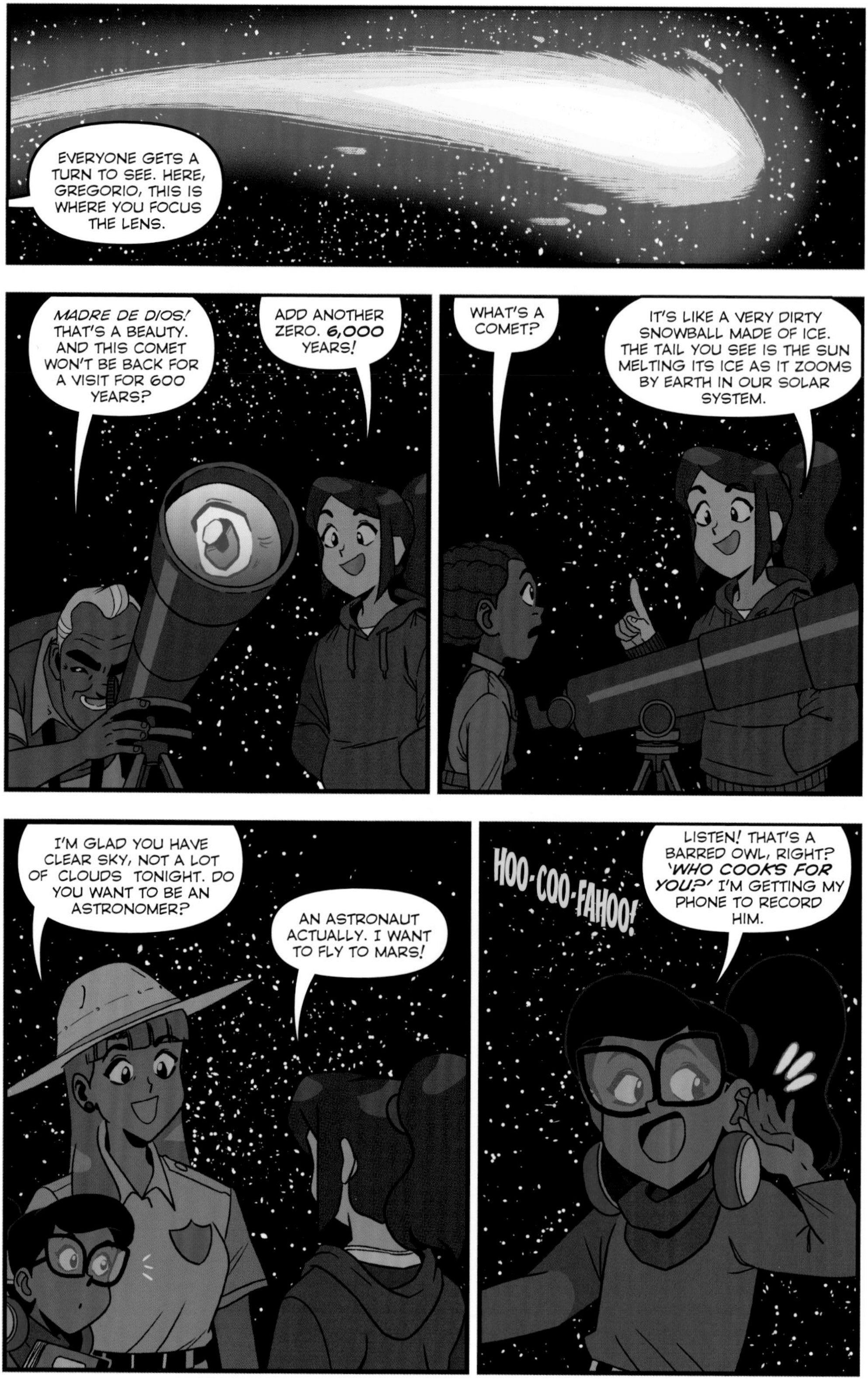

EVERYONE GETS A TURN TO SEE. HERE, GREGORIO, THIS IS WHERE YOU FOCUS THE LENS.
MADRE DE DIOS! THAT'S A BEAUTY. AND THIS COMET WON'T BE BACK FOR A VISIT FOR 600 YEARS?
ADD ANOTHER ZERO. 6,000 YEARS!
WHAT'S A COMET?
IT'S LIKE A VERY DIRTY SNOWBALL MADE OF ICE. THE TAIL YOU SEE IS THE SUN MELTING ITS ICE AS IT ZOOMS BY EARTH IN OUR SOLAR SYSTEM.
I'M GLAD YOU HAVE CLEAR SKY, NOT A LOT OF CLOUDS TONIGHT. DO YOU WANT TO BE AN ASTRONOMER?
AN ASTRONAUT ACTUALLY. I WANT TO FLY TO MARS!
HOO-COO-FAHOO!
LISTEN! THAT'S A BARRED OWL, RIGHT? 'WHO COOKS FOR YOU?' I'M GETTING MY PHONE TO RECORD HIM.

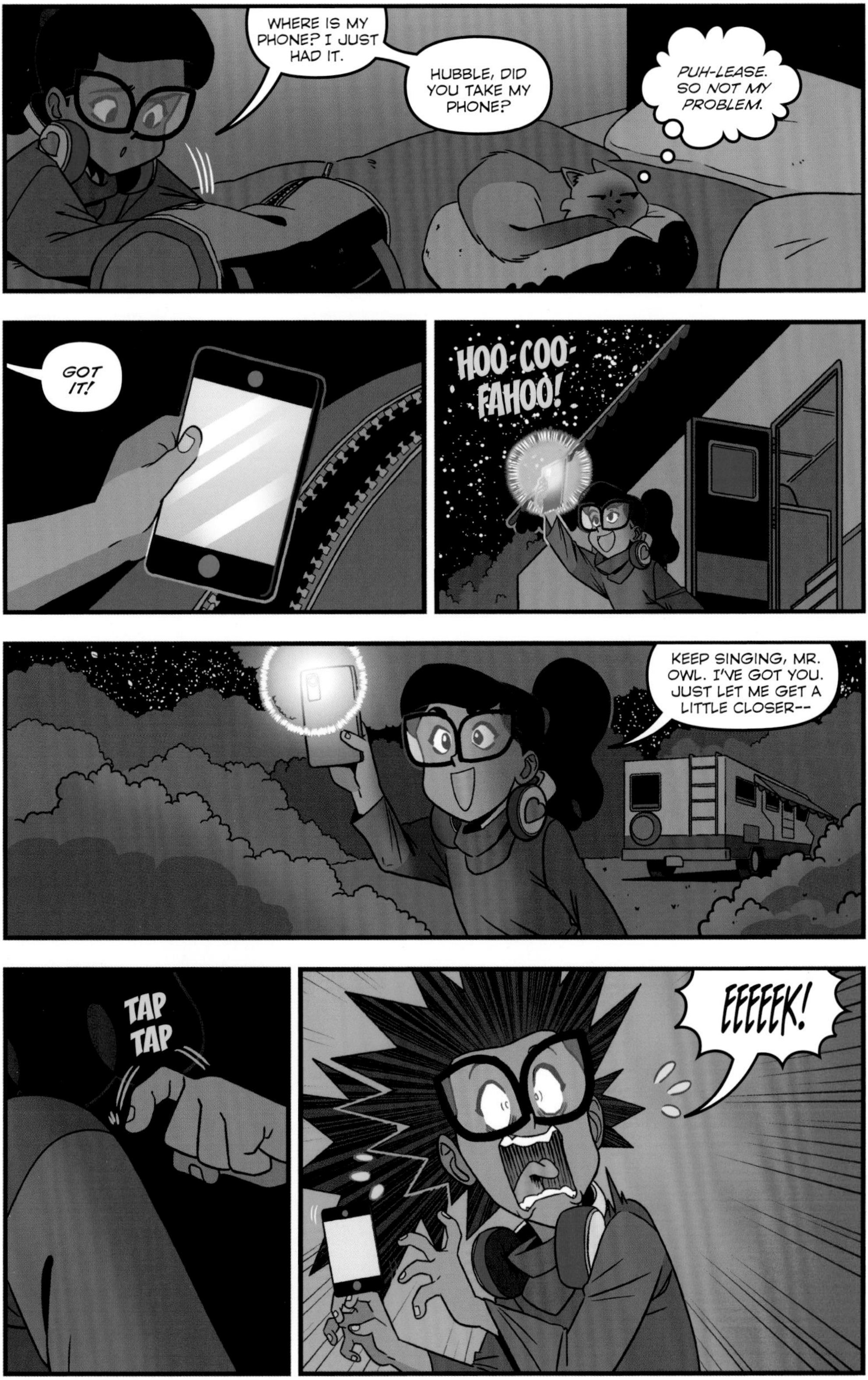
WHERE IS MY PHONE? I JUST HAD IT.
HUBBLE, DID YOU TAKE MY PHONE?
PUH-LEASE. SO NOT MY PROBLEM.
GOT IT!
HOO-COO-FAHOO!
KEEP SINGING, MR. OWL. I'VE GOT YOU. JUST LET ME GET A LITTLE CLOSER--
TAP TAP
EEEEEK!

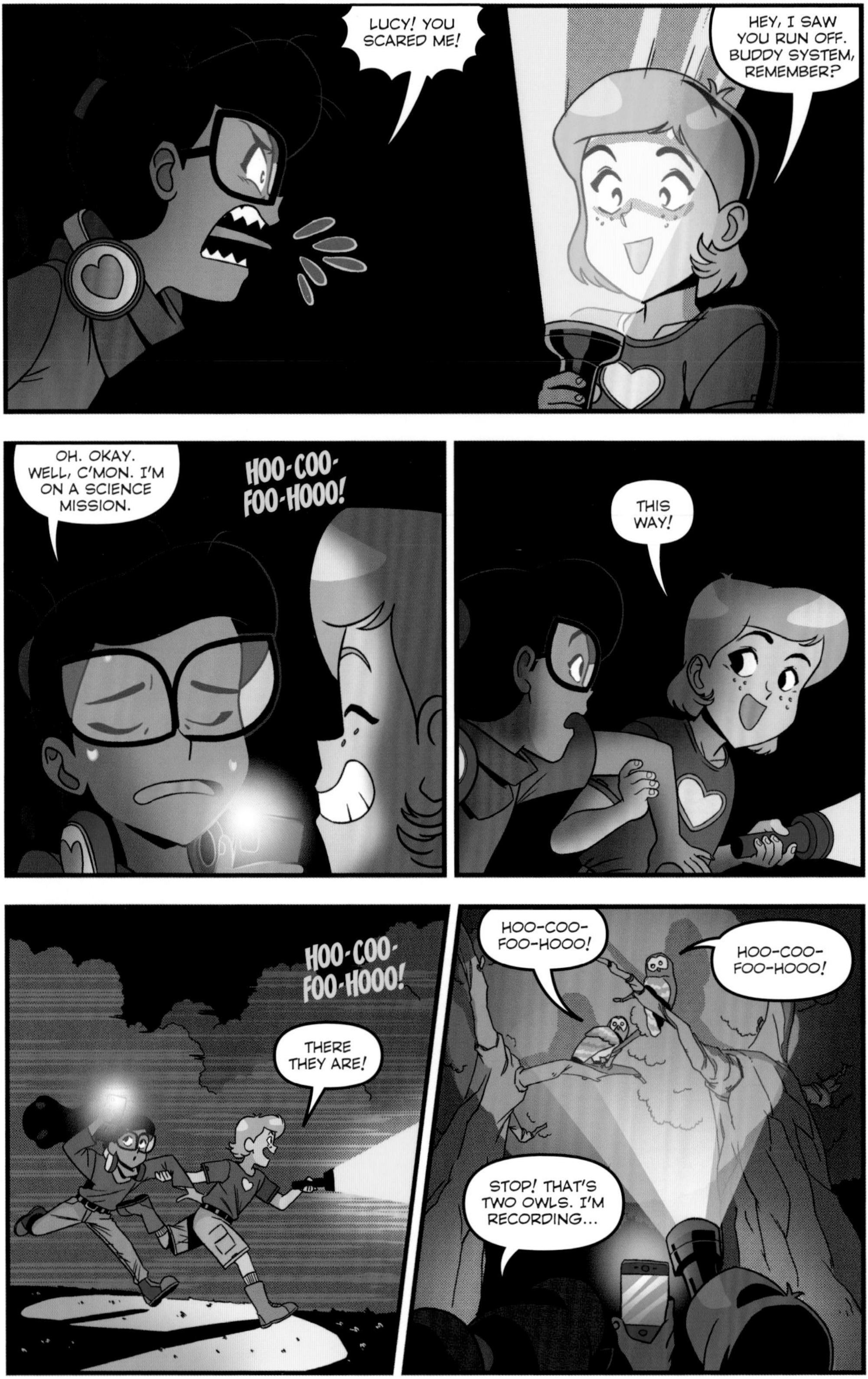
LUCY! YOU SCARED ME!
HEY, I SAW YOU RUN OFF. BUDDY SYSTEM, REMEMBER?
OH. OKAY. WELL, C'MON. I'M ON A SCIENCE MISSION.
HOO-COO-FOO-HOOO!
THIS WAY!
HOO-COO-FOO-HOOO!
THERE THEY ARE!
HOO-COO-FOO-HOOO!
HOO-COO-FOO-HOOO!
STOP! THAT'S TWO OWLS. I'M RECORDING...

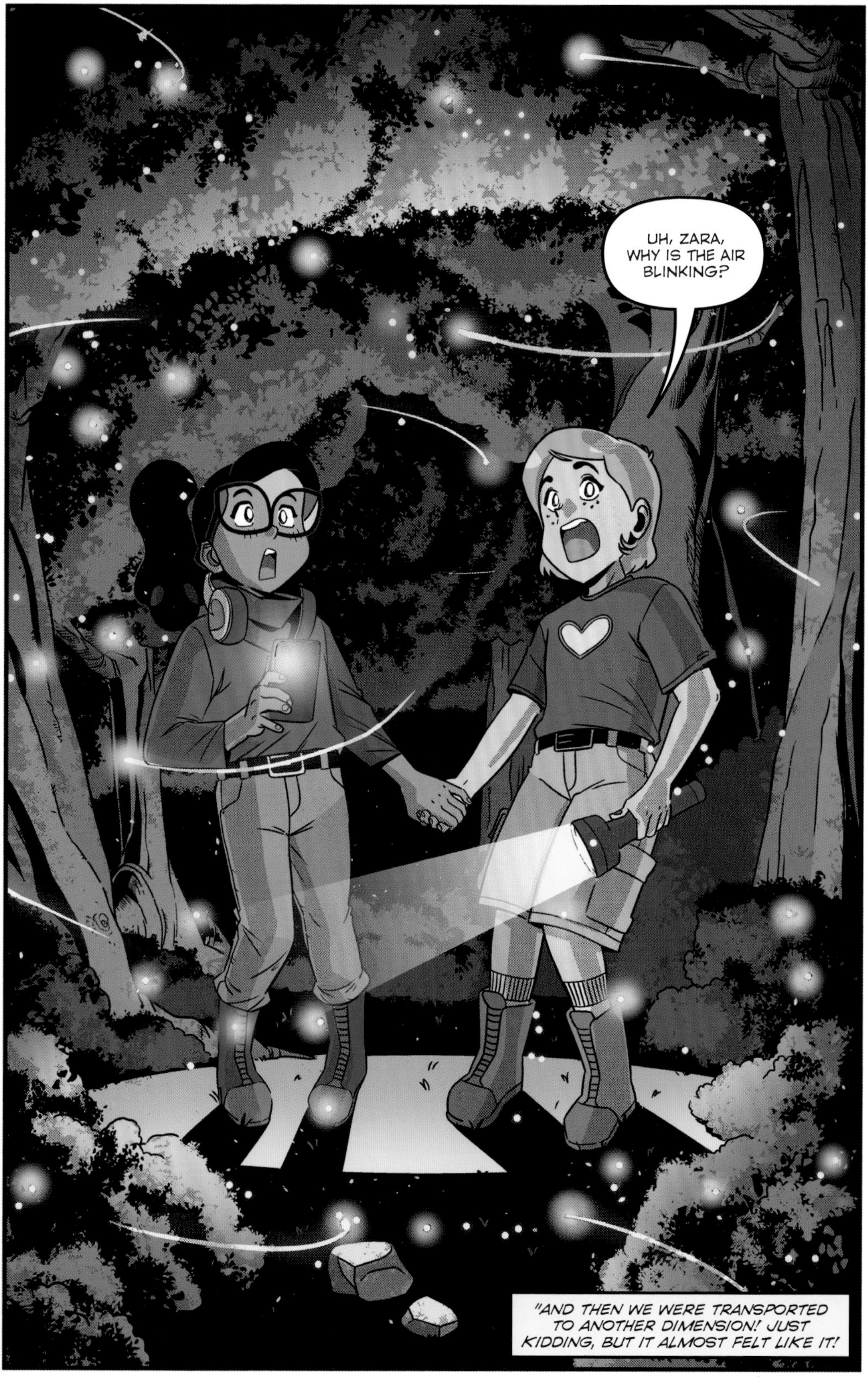
UH, ZARA, WHY IS THE AIR BLINKING?
"AND THEN WE WERE TRANSPORTED TO ANOTHER DIMENSION! JUST KIDDING, BUT IT ALMOST FELT LIKE IT!

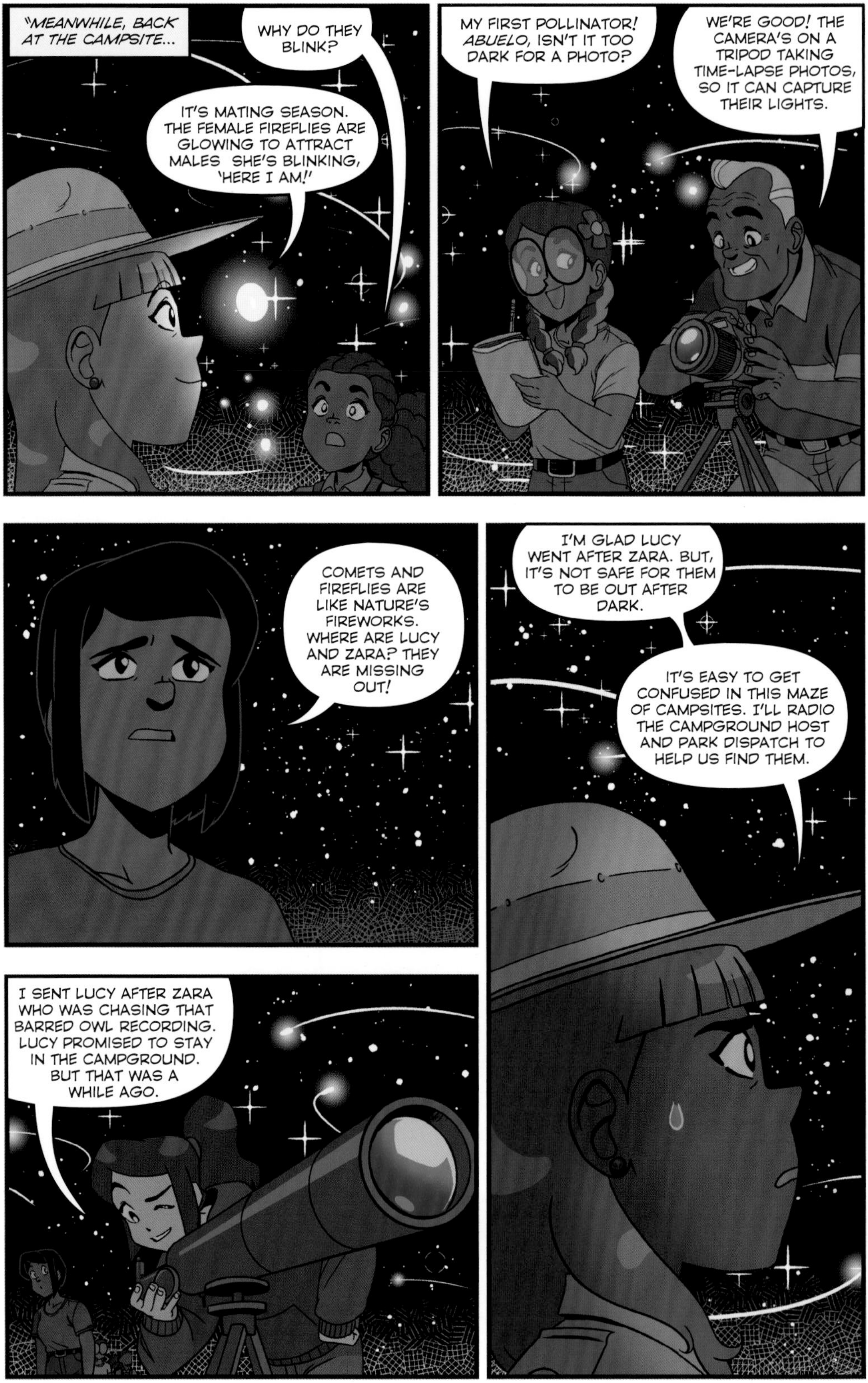
"MEANWHILE, BACK AT THE CAMPSITE...
WHY DO THEY BLINK?
IT'S MATING SEASON. THE FEMALE FIREFLIES ARE GLOWING TO ATTRACT MALES SHE'S BLINKING, 'HERE I AM!'
MY FIRST POLLINATOR! ABUELO, ISN'T IT TOO DARK FOR A PHOTO?
WE'RE GOOD! THE CAMERA'S ON A TRIPOD TAKING TIME-LAPSE PHOTOS, SO IT CAN CAPTURE THEIR LIGHTS.
COMETS AND FIREFLIES ARE LIKE NATURE'S FIREWORKS. WHERE ARE LUCY AND ZARA? THEY ARE MISSING OUT!
I'M GLAD LUCY WENT AFTER ZARA. BUT, IT'S NOT SAFE FOR THEM TO BE OUT AFTER DARK.
IT'S EASY TO GET CONFUSED IN THIS MAZE OF CAMPSITES. I'LL RADIO THE CAMPGROUND HOST AND PARK DISPATCH TO HELP US FIND THEM.
I SENT LUCY AFTER ZARA WHO WAS CHASING THAT BARRED OWL RECORDING. LUCY PROMISED TO STAY IN THE CAMPGROUND. BUT THAT WAS A WHILE AGO.

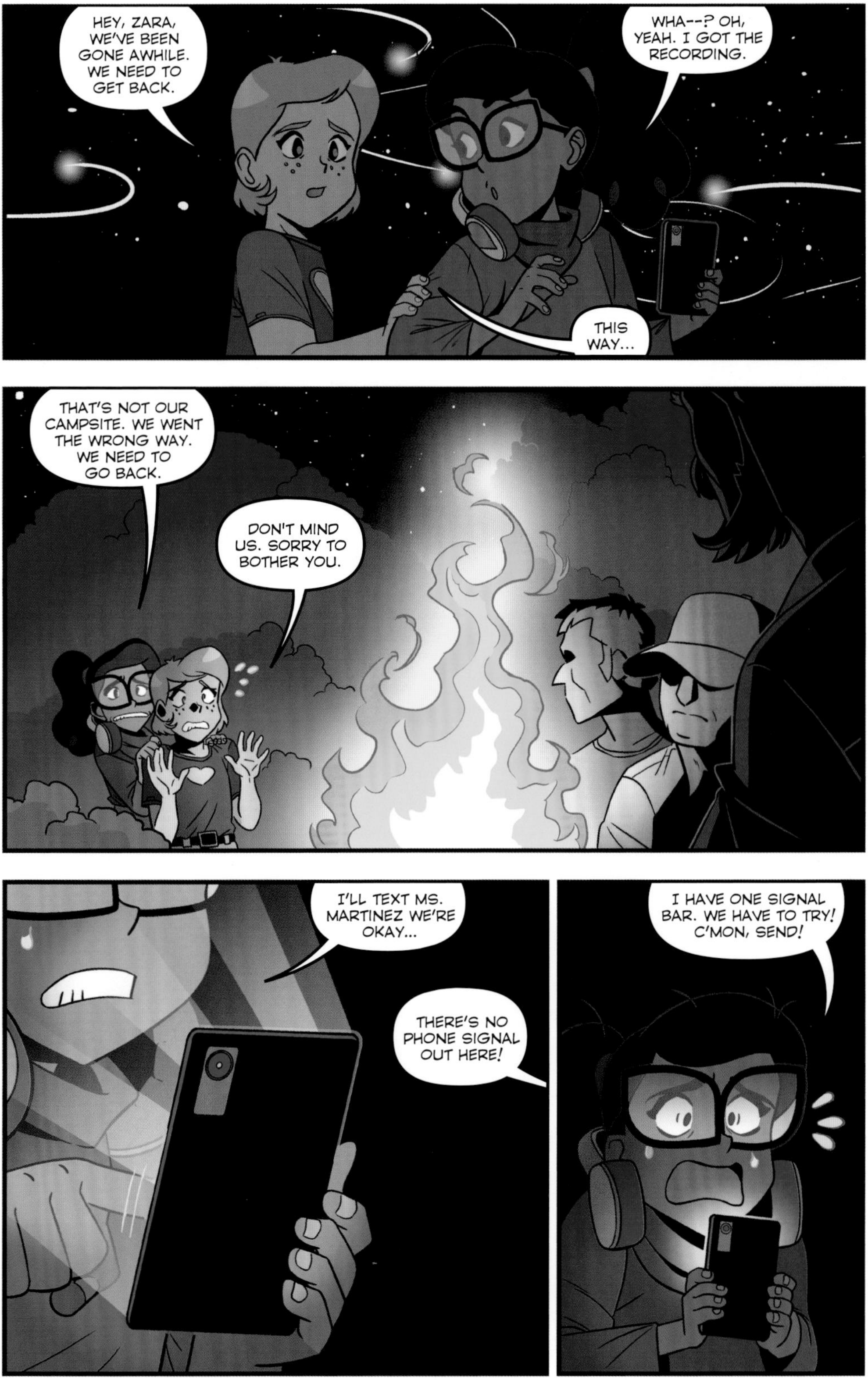
HEY, ZARA, WE'VE BEEN GONE AWHILE. WE NEED TO GET BACK.
WHA--? OH, YEAH. I GOT THE RECORDING.
THIS WAY...
THAT'S NOT OUR CAMPSITE. WE WENT THE WRONG WAY. WE NEED TO GO BACK.
DON'T MIND US. SORRY TO BOTHER YOU.
I'LL TEXT MS. MARTINEZ WE'RE OKAY...
THERE'S NO PHONE SIGNAL OUT HERE!
I HAVE ONE SIGNAL BAR. WE HAVE TO TRY! C'MON, SEND!

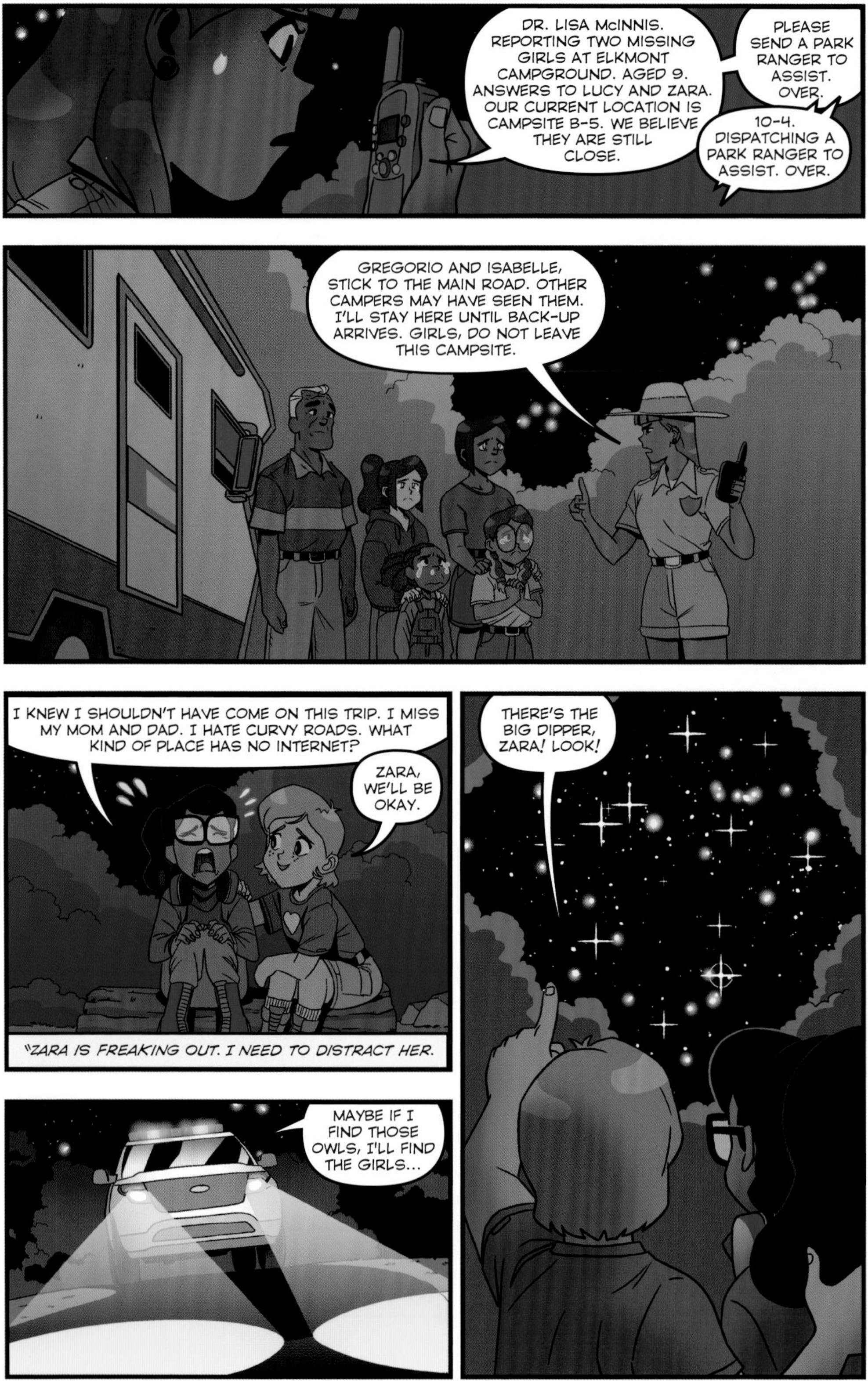
DR. LISA McINNIS. REPORTING TWO MISSING GIRLS AT ELKMONT CAMPGROUND. AGED 9. ANSWERS TO LUCY AND ZARA. OUR CURRENT LOCATION IS CAMPSITE B-5. WE BELIEVE THEY ARE STILL CLOSE.
PLEASE SEND A PARK RANGER TO ASSIST. OVER.
10-4. DISPATCHING A PARK RANGER TO ASSIST. OVER.
GREGORIO AND ISABELLE, STICK TO THE MAIN ROAD. OTHER CAMPERS MAY HAVE SEEN THEM. I'LL STAY HERE UNTIL BACK-UP ARRIVES. GIRLS, DO NOT LEAVE THIS CAMPSITE.
I KNEW I SHOULDN'T HAVE COME ON THIS TRIP. I MISS MY MOM AND DAD. I HATE CURVY ROADS. WHAT KIND OF PLACE HAS NO INTERNET?
ZARA, WE'LL BE OKAY.
ZARA IS FREAKING OUT. I NEED TO DISTRACT HER.
MAYBE IF I FIND THOSE OWLS, I'LL FIND THE GIRLS...
THERE'S THE BIG DIPPER, ZARA! LOOK!

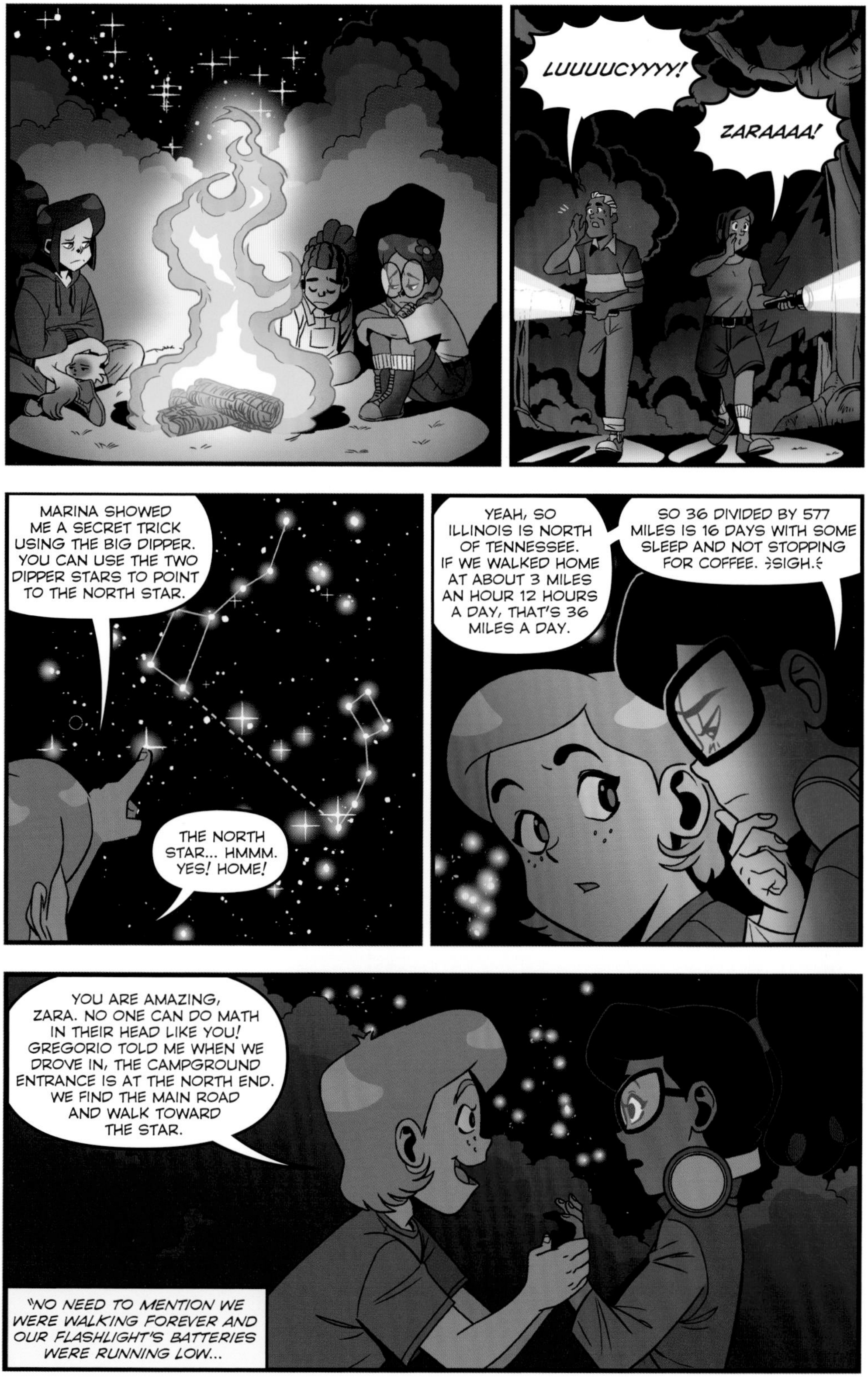
LUUUUCYYYY!
ZARAAAA!
MARINA SHOWED ME A SECRET TRICK USING THE BIG DIPPER. YOU CAN USE THE TWO DIPPER STARS TO POINT TO THE NORTH STAR.
THE NORTH STAR... HMMM. YES! HOME!
YEAH, SO ILLINOIS IS NORTH OF TENNESSEE. IF WE WALKED HOME AT ABOUT 3 MILES AN HOUR 12 HOURS A DAY, THAT'S 36 MILES A DAY.
SO 36 DIVIDED BY 577 MILES IS 16 DAYS WITH SOME SLEEP AND NOT STOPPING FOR COFFEE. ⋺SIGH.⋲
YOU ARE AMAZING, ZARA. NO ONE CAN DO MATH IN THEIR HEAD LIKE YOU! GREGORIO TOLD ME WHEN WE DROVE IN, THE CAMPGROUND ENTRANCE IS AT THE NORTH END. WE FIND THE MAIN ROAD AND WALK TOWARD THE STAR.
"NO NEED TO MENTION WE WERE WALKING FOREVER AND OUR FLASHLIGHT'S BATTERIES WERE RUNNING LOW...

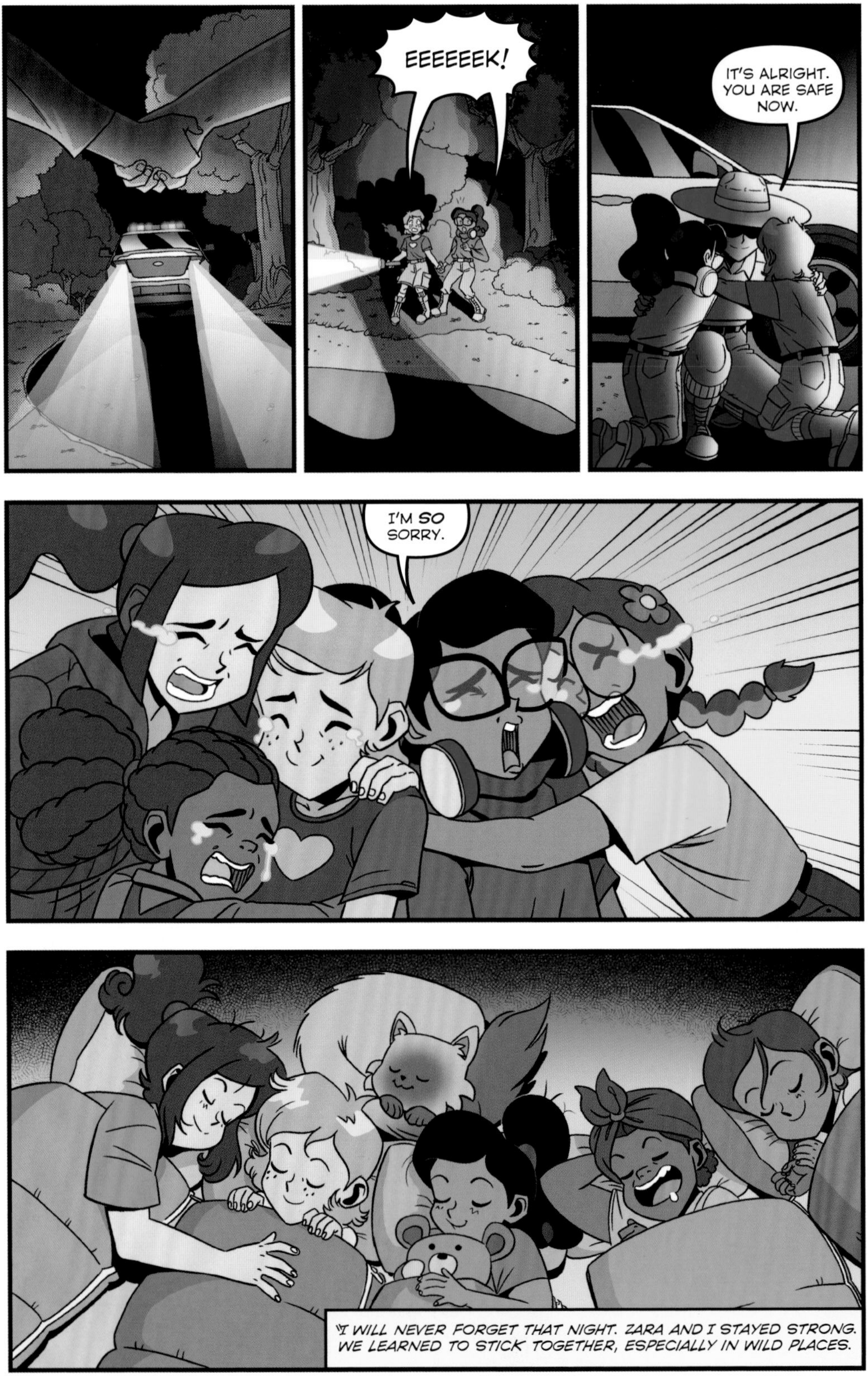
EEEEEEK!
IT'S ALRIGHT. YOU ARE SAFE NOW.
I'M SO SORRY.
"I WILL NEVER FORGET THAT NIGHT. ZARA AND I STAYED STRONG. WE LEARNED TO STICK TOGETHER, ESPECIALLY IN WILD PLACES.

CHAPTER EIGHT: THE GOOD OLD DAYS

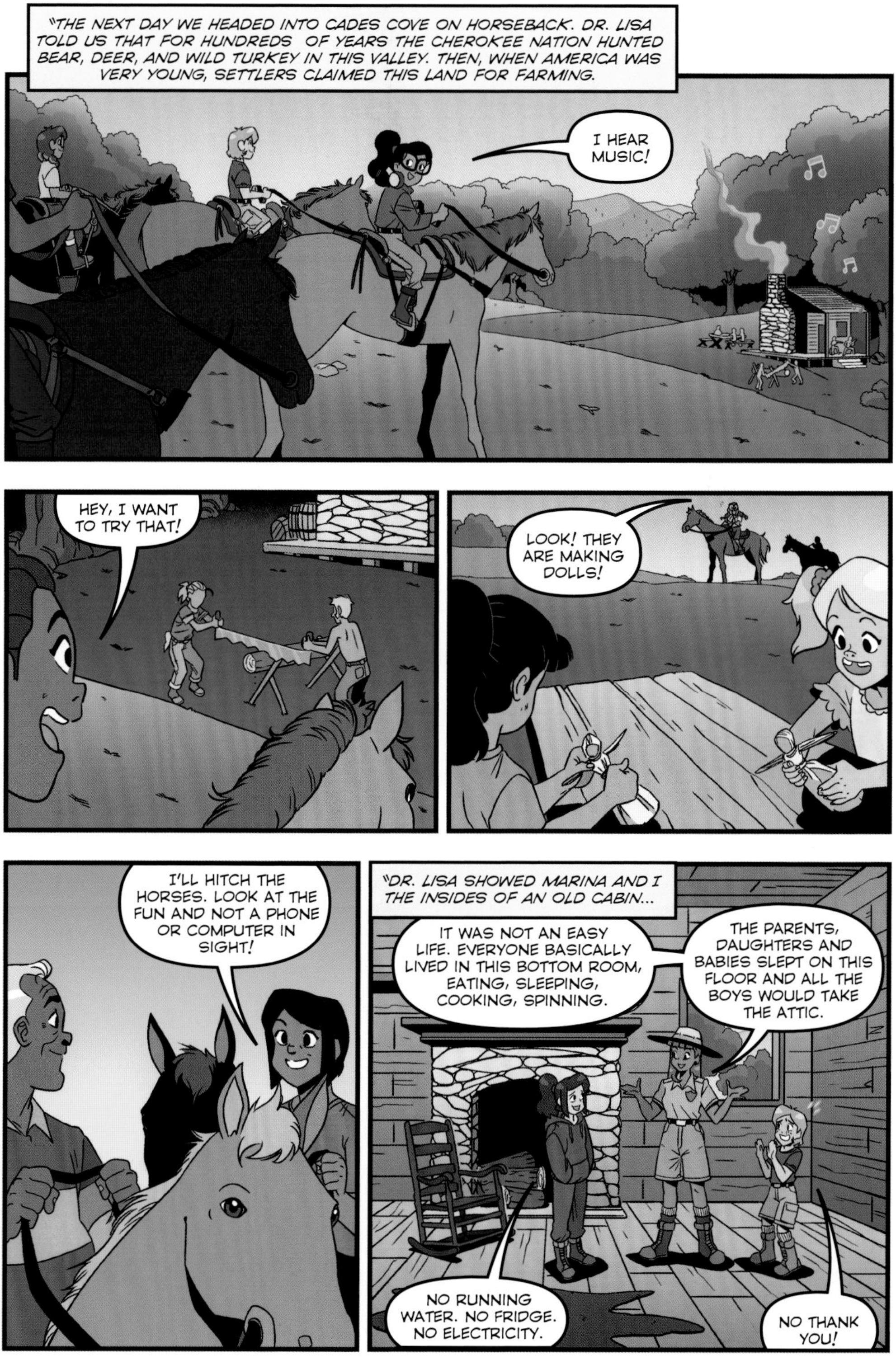
"THE NEXT DAY WE HEADED INTO CADES COVE ON HORSEBACK. DR. LISA TOLD US THAT FOR HUNDREDS OF YEARS THE CHEROKEE NATION HUNTED BEAR, DEER, AND WILD TURKEY IN THIS VALLEY. THEN, WHEN AMERICA WAS VERY YOUNG, SETTLERS CLAIMED THIS LAND FOR FARMING.
I HEAR MUSIC!
HEY, I WANT TO TRY THAT!
LOOK! THEY ARE MAKING DOLLS!
I'LL HITCH THE HORSES. LOOK AT THE FUN AND NOT A PHONE OR COMPUTER IN SIGHT!
"DR. LISA SHOWED MARINA AND I THE INSIDES OF AN OLD CABIN...
IT WAS NOT AN EASY LIFE. EVERYONE BASICALLY LIVED IN THIS BOTTOM ROOM, EATING, SLEEPING, COOKING, SPINNING.
THE PARENTS, DAUGHTERS AND BABIES SLEPT ON THIS FLOOR AND ALL THE BOYS WOULD TAKE THE ATTIC.
NO RUNNING WATER. NO FRIDGE. NO ELECTRICITY.
NO THANK YOU!

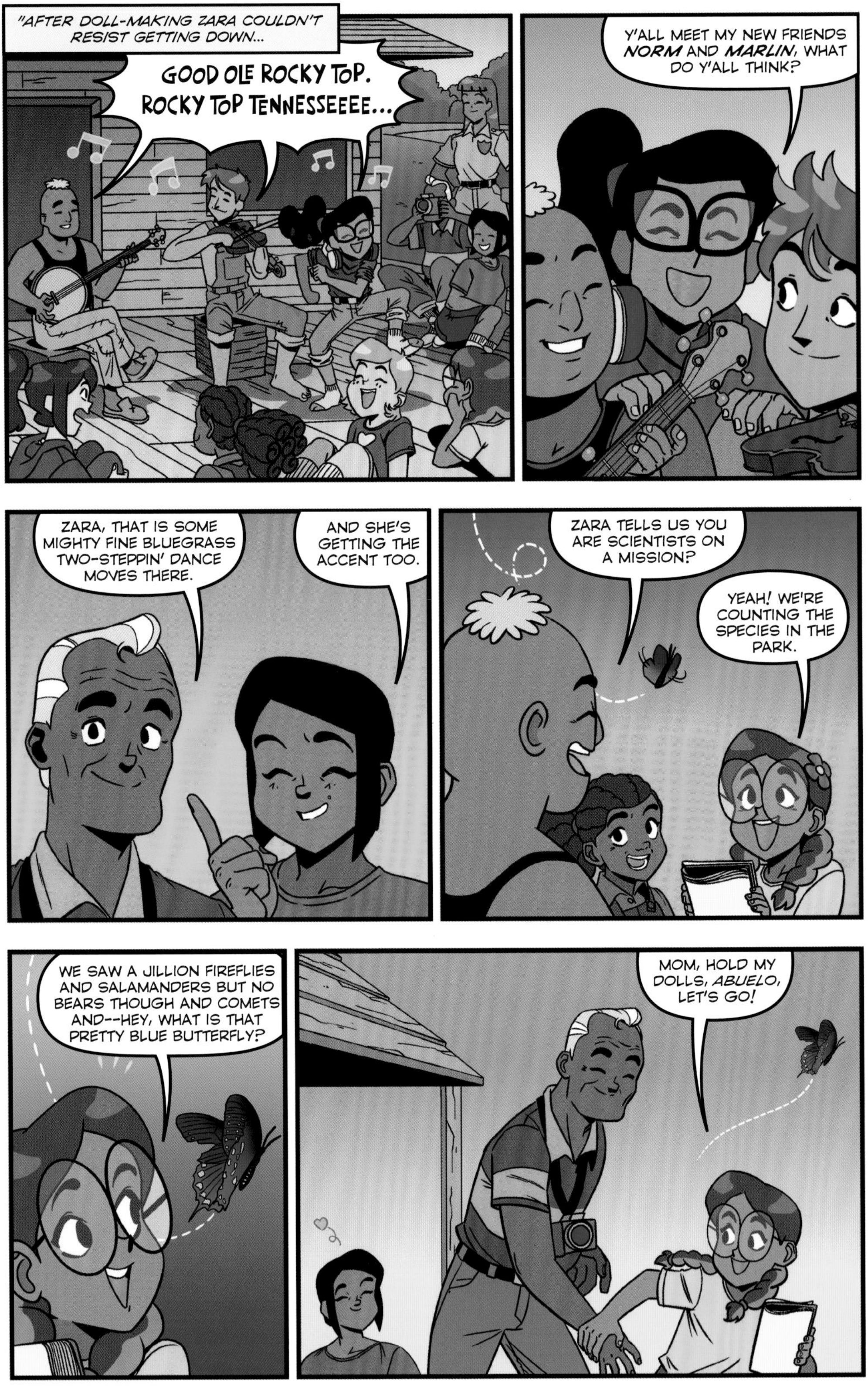
"AFTER DOLL-MAKING ZARA COULDN'T RESIST GETTING DOWN...
GOOD OLE ROCKY TOP. ROCKY TOP TENNESSEEEE...
Y'ALL MEET MY NEW FRIENDS NORM AND MARLIN, WHAT DO Y'ALL THINK?
ZARA, THAT IS SOME MIGHTY FINE BLUEGRASS TWO-STEPPIN' DANCE MOVES THERE.
AND SHE'S GETTING THE ACCENT TOO.
ZARA TELLS US YOU ARE SCIENTISTS ON A MISSION?
YEAH! WE'RE COUNTING THE SPECIES IN THE PARK.
WE SAW A JILLION FIREFLIES AND SALAMANDERS BUT NO BEARS THOUGH AND COMETS AND--HEY, WHAT IS THAT PRETTY BLUE BUTTERFLY?
MOM, HOLD MY DOLLS, ABUELO, LET'S GO!

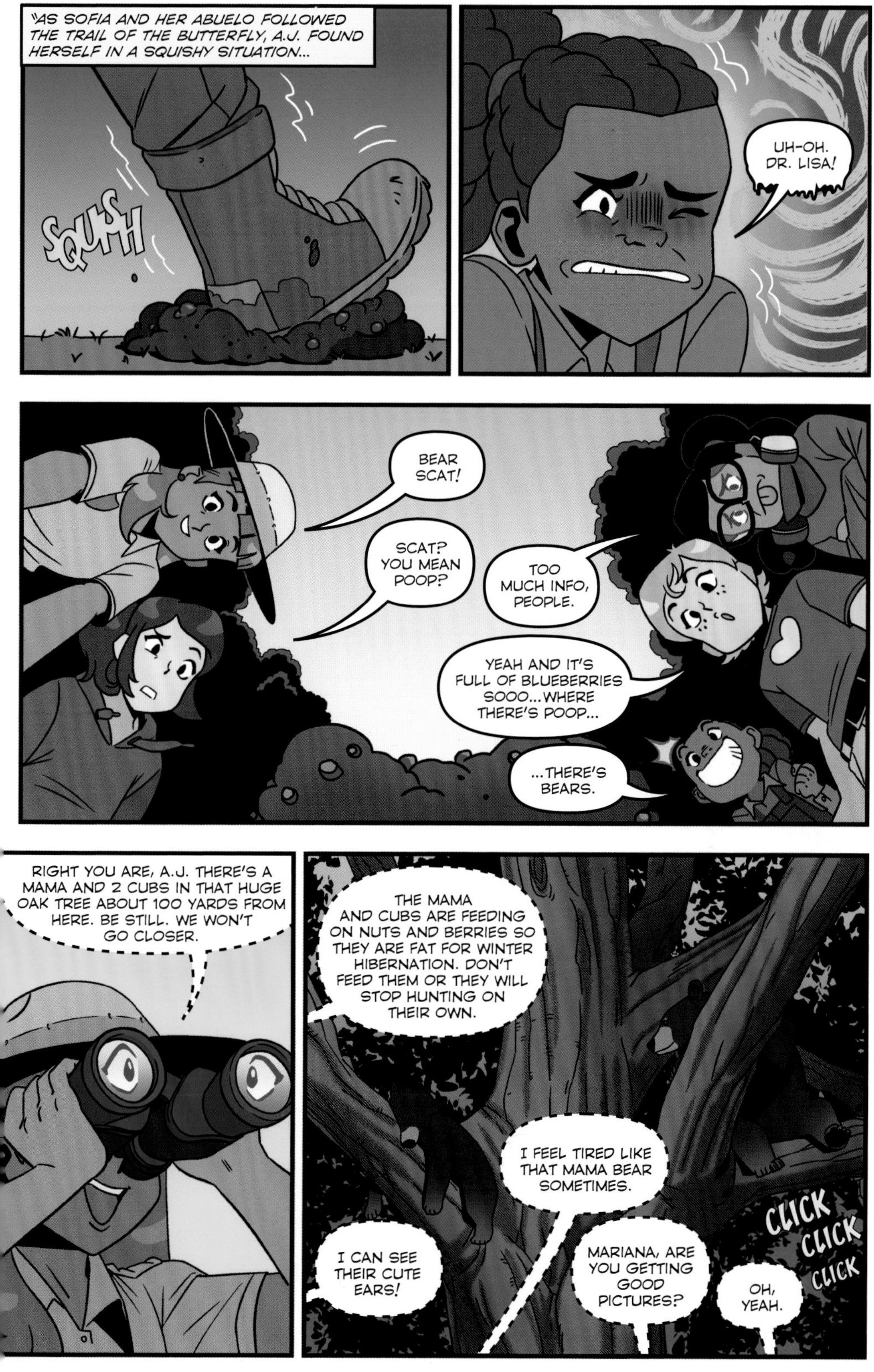
AS SOFIA AND HER ABUELO FOLLOWED THE TRAIL OF THE BUTTERFLY, A.J. FOUND HERSELF IN A SQUISHY SITUATION...
SQUISH
UH-OH. DR. LISA!
BEAR SCAT!
SCAT? YOU MEAN POOP?
TOO MUCH INFO, PEOPLE.
YEAH AND IT'S FULL OF BLUEBERRIES SOOO...WHERE THERE'S POOP...
...THERE'S BEARS.
RIGHT YOU ARE, A.J. THERE'S A MAMA AND 2 CUBS IN THAT HUGE OAK TREE ABOUT 100 YARDS FROM HERE. BE STILL. WE WON'T GO CLOSER.
THE MAMA AND CUBS ARE FEEDING ON NUTS AND BERRIES SO THEY ARE FAT FOR WINTER HIBERNATION. DON'T FEED THEM OR THEY WILL STOP HUNTING ON THEIR OWN.
I FEEL TIRED LIKE THAT MAMA BEAR SOMETIMES.
I CAN SEE THEIR CUTE EARS!
MARIANA, ARE YOU GETTING GOOD PICTURES?
CLICK CLICK CLICK
OH, YEAH.

CHAPTER NINE: TREE HUGGERS

"IT HAD BEEN A PERFECT DAY. SOFIA, GREGORIO, AND I WERE BUSY ORGANIZING ALL THE SPECIES WE SPOTTED AND THEIR LOCATIONS SINCE HIS CAMERA RECORDED LONGITUDE AND LATITUDE. WHEN WE GOT A STRONG SIGNAL, SOFIA WOULD UPLOAD OUR DATA ON A CITIZEN SCIENTIST PHONE APP.

WOW. WE SAW SPICEBUSH AND ZEBRA SWALLOWTAILS AND MONARCHS. FOR FLOWERS, I'LL LOG CONEFLOWERS, BEE BALM, QUEEN ANNE'S LACE. LOCATION?

CADES COVE, TENNESSEE. LONGITUDE: 35 DEGREES, 35 MINUTES NORTH. LATITUDE: 83 DEGREES, 50 MINUTES WEST.

DON'T FORGET THE BLACK BEARS!

GIRLS, IT'S GETTING LATE. TOMORROW IS OUR LAST DAY AND THEN WE'LL NEED TO PACK FOR HOME. LET'S HIT THE HAY FOR ONE MORE BIG DAY!

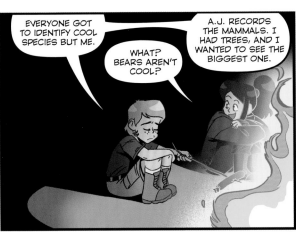

EVERYONE GOT TO IDENTIFY COOL SPECIES BUT ME.

WHAT? BEARS AREN'T COOL?

A.J. RECORDS THE MAMMALS. I HAD TREES, AND I WANTED TO SEE THE BIGGEST ONE.

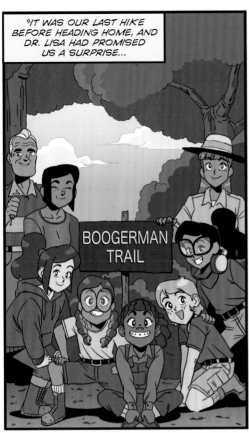

"IT WAS OUR LAST HIKE BEFORE HEADING HOME, AND DR. LISA HAD PROMISED US A SURPRISE...

BOOGERMAN TRAIL

THE STORY GOES THAT A YOUNG PIONEER WHO LIVED HERE TOLD HIS TEACHER HE WANTED TO BE A 'BOOGERMAN' WHEN HE GREW UP!

HA HA HA!

"THE BRIDGES WERE FUN, BUT EVEN COOLER, WHEN THEY WASH OUT.

TIME TO ROLL UP THOSE PANTS!

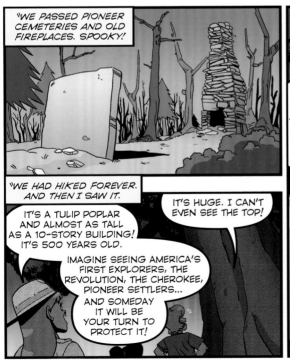

"WE PASSED PIONEER CEMETERIES AND OLD FIREPLACES. SPOOKY!

"WE HAD HIKED FOREVER. AND THEN I SAW IT.

IT'S A TULIP POPLAR AND ALMOST AS TALL AS A 10-STORY BUILDING! IT'S 500 YEARS OLD.

IT'S HUGE. I CAN'T EVEN SEE THE TOP!

IMAGINE SEEING AMERICA'S FIRST EXPLORERS, THE REVOLUTION, THE CHEROKEE, PIONEER SETTLERS... AND SOMEDAY IT WILL BE YOUR TURN TO PROTECT IT!

ME? PROTECT IT? I LIVE ALMOST 1,000 MILES FROM HERE.

YOU CAN PROTECT THE SMOKIES NO MATTER WHERE YOU LIVE. PLANTING POLLINATOR GARDENS HELPS THE MONARCHS. AND PLANTING TREES AT HOME CLEANS THE WATER AND AIR. WE MUST ALL DO OUR PART. THIS PARK, THIS TREE, CONNECTS ALL OF US.

CAN I HUG IT NOW?

"THE TREE WAS SO BIG, IT TOOK ALL OF US TO GIVE IT A GOOD HUG...

"I LOVE BEING BACK HOME, BUT I MISS THE SMOKIES SO MUCH. BUT MAYBE SOMEDAY I WILL BE A SCIENTIST LIKE DR. LISA, SAVING OUR PLANET FOREVER.

WHA--?

BUZZZ

COME OVER! ABUELO SAYS IT'S TIME!

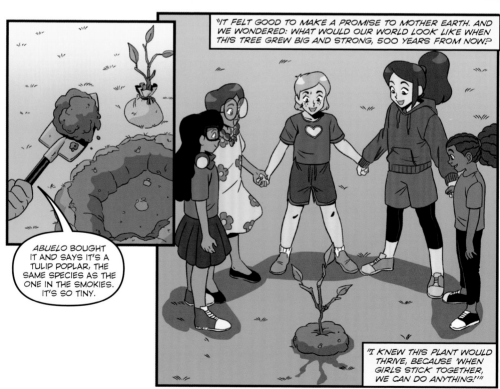

"IT FELT GOOD TO MAKE A PROMISE TO MOTHER EARTH. AND WE WONDERED: WHAT WOULD OUR WORLD LOOK LIKE WHEN THIS TREE GREW BIG AND STRONG, 500 YEARS FROM NOW?

ABUELO BOUGHT IT AND SAYS IT'S A TULIP POPLAR, THE SAME SPECIES AS THE ONE IN THE SMOKIES. IT'S SO TINY.

"I KNEW THIS PLANT WOULD THRIVE, BECAUSE 'WHEN GIRLS STICK TOGETHER, WE CAN DO ANYTHING!'"

WATCH OUT FOR PAPERCUTZ

Welcome to the flora-and-fauna-filled fifth GEEKY F@B 5 graphic novel, "Smoky Mountain Science Squad," by Lucy & Liz Lareau, our daughter & mother writing team and Ryan Jampole, our award-winning artist, brought to you by Papercutz, the campy cut-ups dedicated to publishing great graphic novels for all ages. I'm Jim Salicrup, the Editor-in-Chief and Park Enthusiast, here to ramble about a different type of park, So, park your carcass and make yourself comfy, 'cause here we go...

The Geeky F@b 5 were lucky enough to hitch a ride with their abuelo Gregorio to one of our country's great National Parks. While I have yet to visit that particular park, I have been driven through the Smoky Mountains, and that can be quite an experience! While driving on those twisting roads high up on the mountains it can get scary when you're surrounded in mist and can barely see more than a few feet in front of you. Luckily, we were able to follow the taillights of the vehicle in front of us and came out of the mists alive.

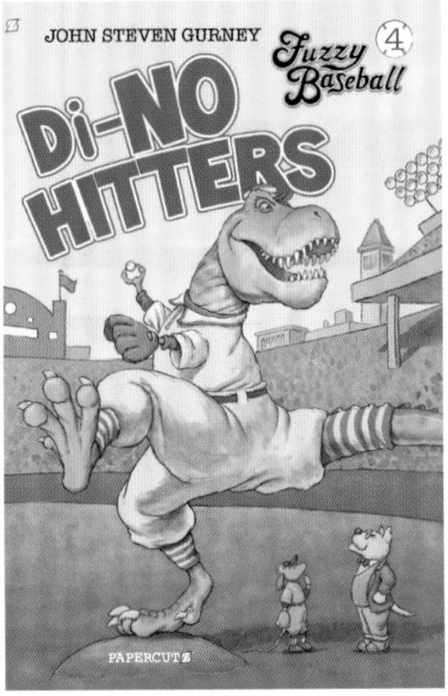
JOHN STEVEN GURNEY
Fuzzy Baseball
4
Di-NO HITTERS
PAPERCUTZ
© 2021 by John Steven Gurney.

Fortunately, Lucy Lareau also survived--see her Letter below. But speaking of parks, our special preview is about a couple of different kinds of parks.

This popular Papercutz graphic novel series combines two of my favorite things from my childhood—the animals from the Bronx Zoo with the sport of baseball as played by the Bronx Bombers in Yankee Stadium. Of course, I'm talking about the Fernwood Valley Fuzzies, who are back in—FUZZY BASEBALL #4 "Di-No Hitters," by John Steven Gurney. If you thought animals playing baseball was a wacky idea, wait till you meet the team they're up against this time—the Triassic Park Titans!

So, find a nice shady spot in the park where you can sit down and enjoy the fun when John Steven Gurney transports us to the imaginary ballpark where Blossom Honey Possum, Bo Grizzly, Sandy Kofox, Jackie Rabbitson, and the rest of the Fuzzies take on the prehistoric players from Triassic Park! Oh, and you may want to take along the next GEEKY F@B 5 graphic novel, coming soon, with you too!

Thanks,

Jim

Letter from LUCY LAREAU

Howdy from the Smoky Mountains! Meet my new friend, Dr. Lisa McInnis, in the cool Smokey the Bear hat and my mates, Josie and Callagh, who help me brainstorm fun ideas for the GF5. For this book, I wanted to do a road trip and take a break from Earhart Elementary, so we headed for the Great Smoky Mountains National Park in Tennessee. Our adventure to the "Smokies" was a road trip like none other. First of all, driving through mountains is one of the most gorgeous and scary things ever. Hint: don't eat donuts before going on those curvy roads! Looking off the edge and seeing nothing but miles of mountains and trees was exhilarating. But the drive was worth it to meet Dr. Lisa McInnis. She leads scientists in the park to protect the bears, the birds, the trees, every living thing! She shared her love for nature with us, and she cares for the trees like they are her children. She is so humble with her work, but you can tell she is extremely smart. After she told us how easy it was to get lost, I never really thought about that until we were on a trail all by ourselves and seeing how dense the forest was. After talking to Dr. Lisa, I appreciated the trip 10x more. Do you like vacations to parks? I learned that we can all enjoy and protect the Smokies, no matter where we live

Peace out,

Lucy

STAY IN TOUCH!

EMAIL:	salicrup@papercutz.com
WEB:	papercutz.com
TWITTER:	@papercutzgn
INSTAGRAM:	@papercutzgn
FACEBOOK:	PAPERCUTZGRAPHICNOVELS
FAN MAIL:	Papercutz, 160 Broadway, Suite 700, East Wing, New York, NY 10038

Go to papercutz.com and sign up for the free Papercutz e-newsletter!

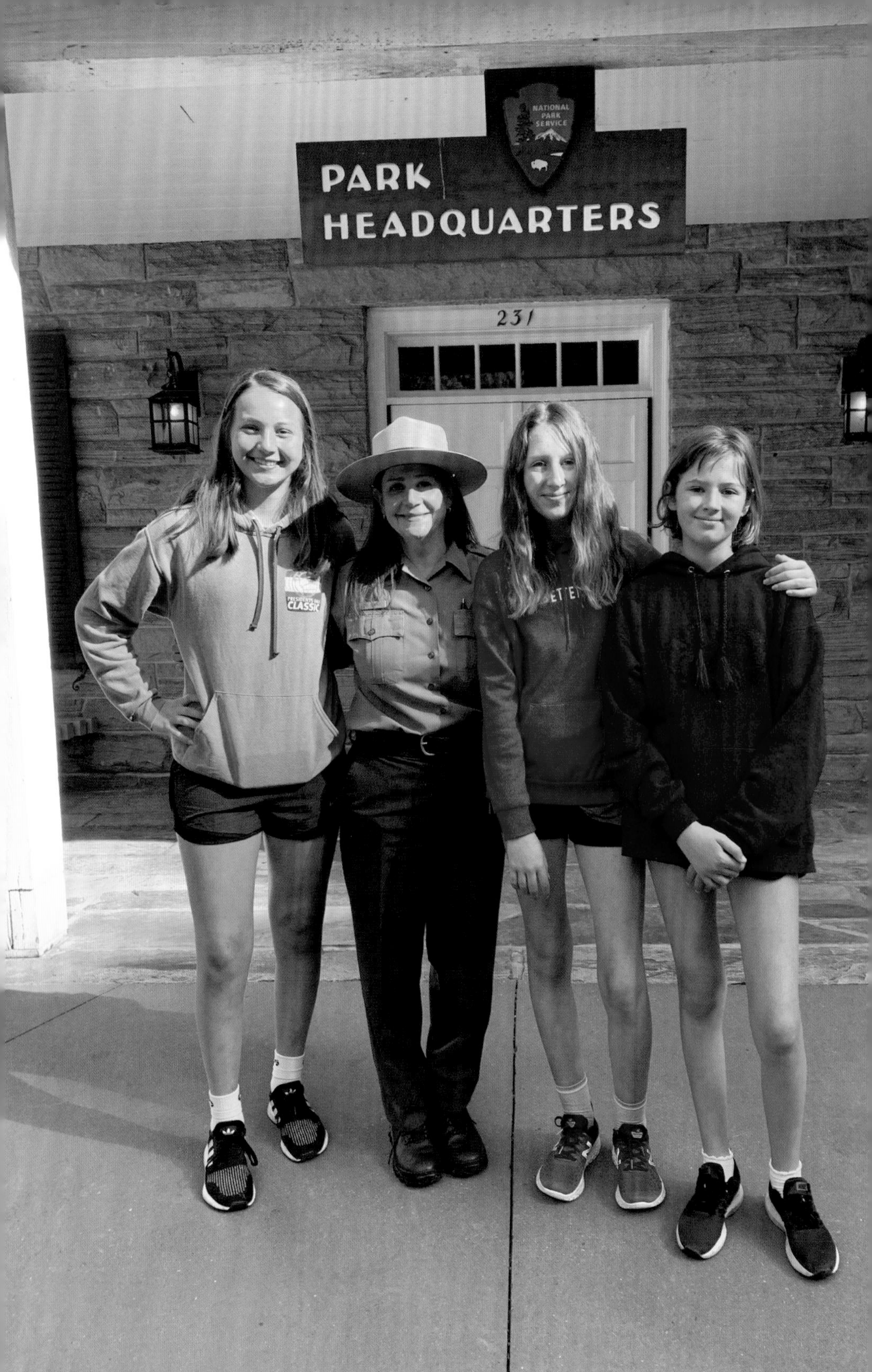
NATIONAL PARK SERVICE
PARK HEADQUARTERS
231
CLASSIC

Left to right: GF5 Co-author Lucy Lareau, Dr. Lisa McInnis, Josie and Callagh Sheehan.

Special Preview of FUZZY BASEBALL #4 "Di-No Hitters"...

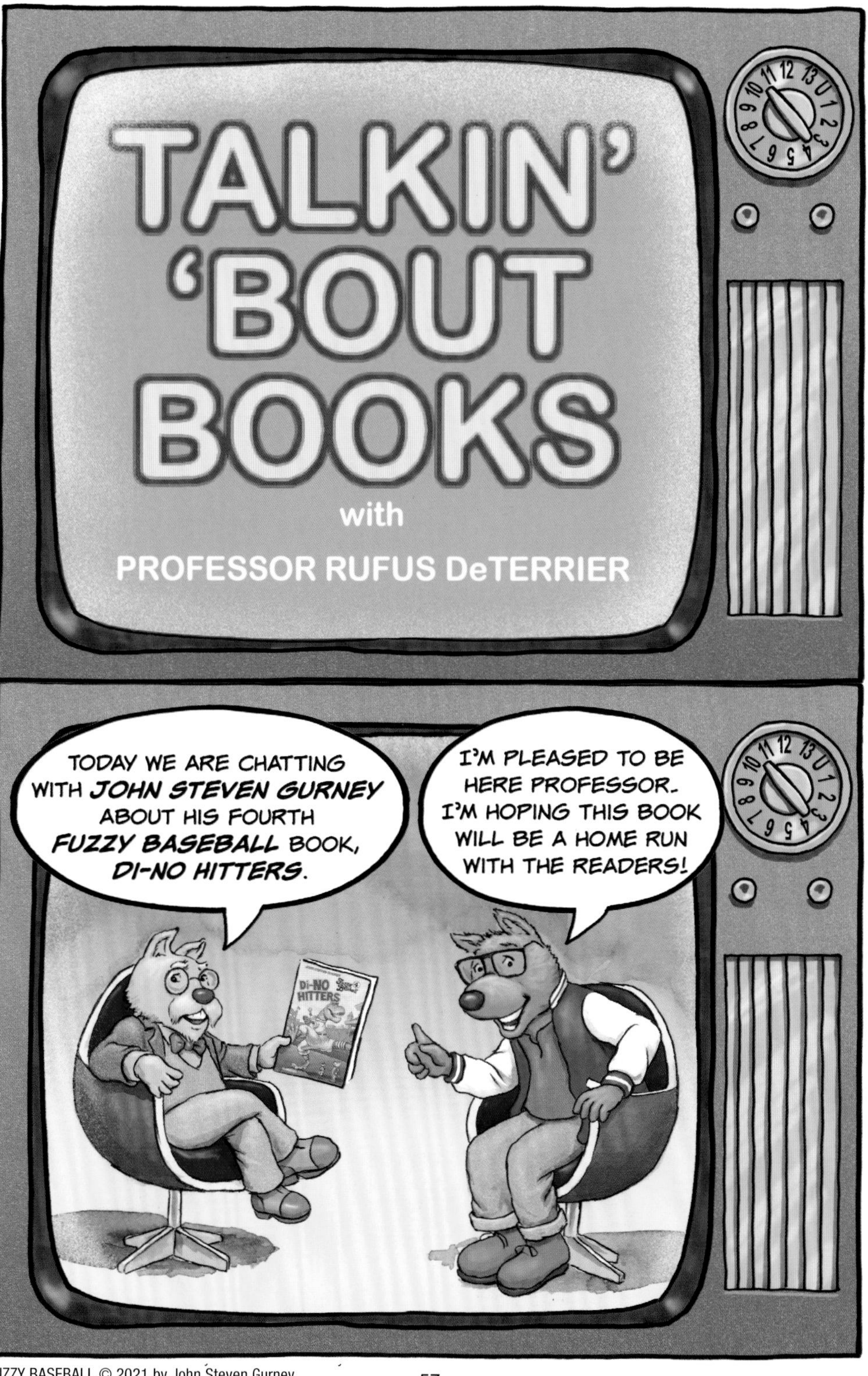
TALKIN' 'BOUT BOOKS
with
PROFESSOR RUFUS DeTERRIER
TODAY WE ARE CHATTING WITH JOHN STEVEN GURNEY ABOUT HIS FOURTH FUZZY BASEBALL BOOK, DI-NO HITTERS.
I'M PLEASED TO BE HERE PROFESSOR. I'M HOPING THIS BOOK WILL BE A HOME RUN WITH THE READERS!

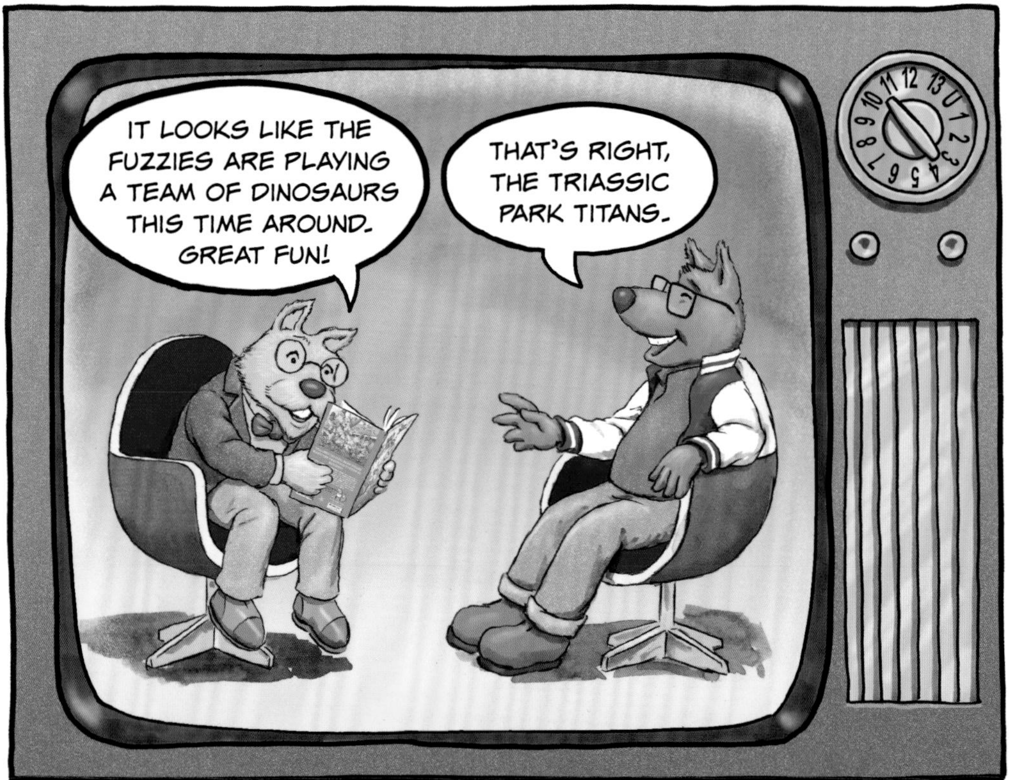
IT LOOKS LIKE THE FUZZIES ARE PLAYING A TEAM OF DINOSAURS THIS TIME AROUND. GREAT FUN!
THAT'S RIGHT, THE TRIASSIC PARK TITANS.

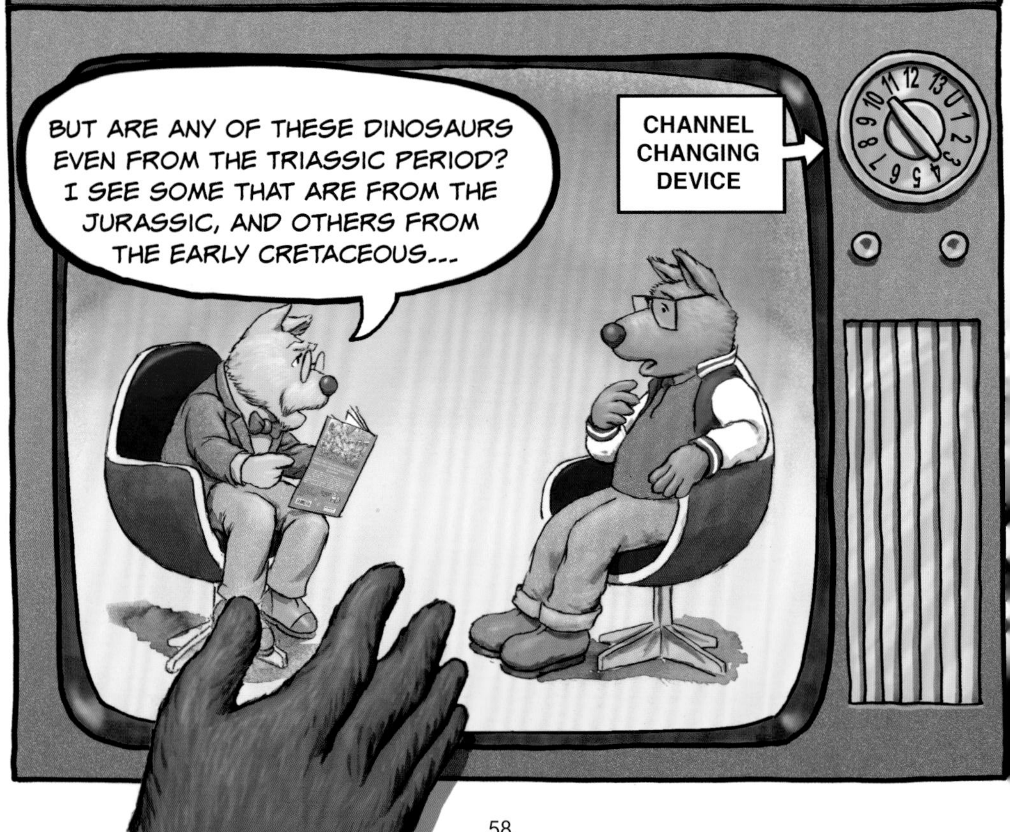
BUT ARE ANY OF THESE DINOSAURS EVEN FROM THE TRIASSIC PERIOD? I SEE SOME THAT ARE FROM THE JURASSIC, AND OTHERS FROM THE EARLY CRETACEOUS...
CHANNEL CHANGING DEVICE

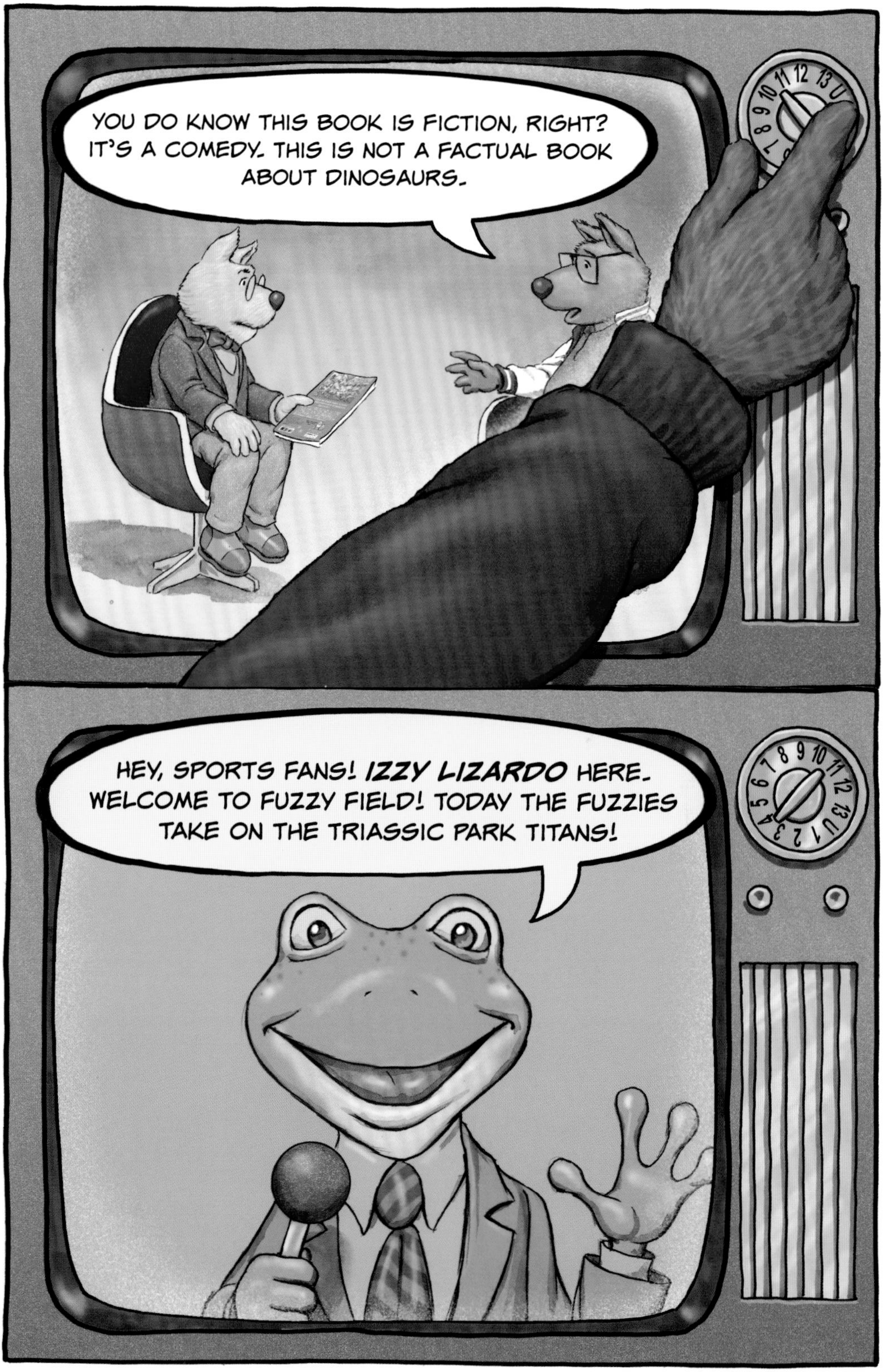
YOU DO KNOW THIS BOOK IS FICTION, RIGHT? IT'S A COMEDY. THIS IS NOT A FACTUAL BOOK ABOUT DINOSAURS.
HEY, SPORTS FANS! *IZZY LIZARDO* HERE. WELCOME TO FUZZY FIELD! TODAY THE FUZZIES TAKE ON THE TRIASSIC PARK TITANS!

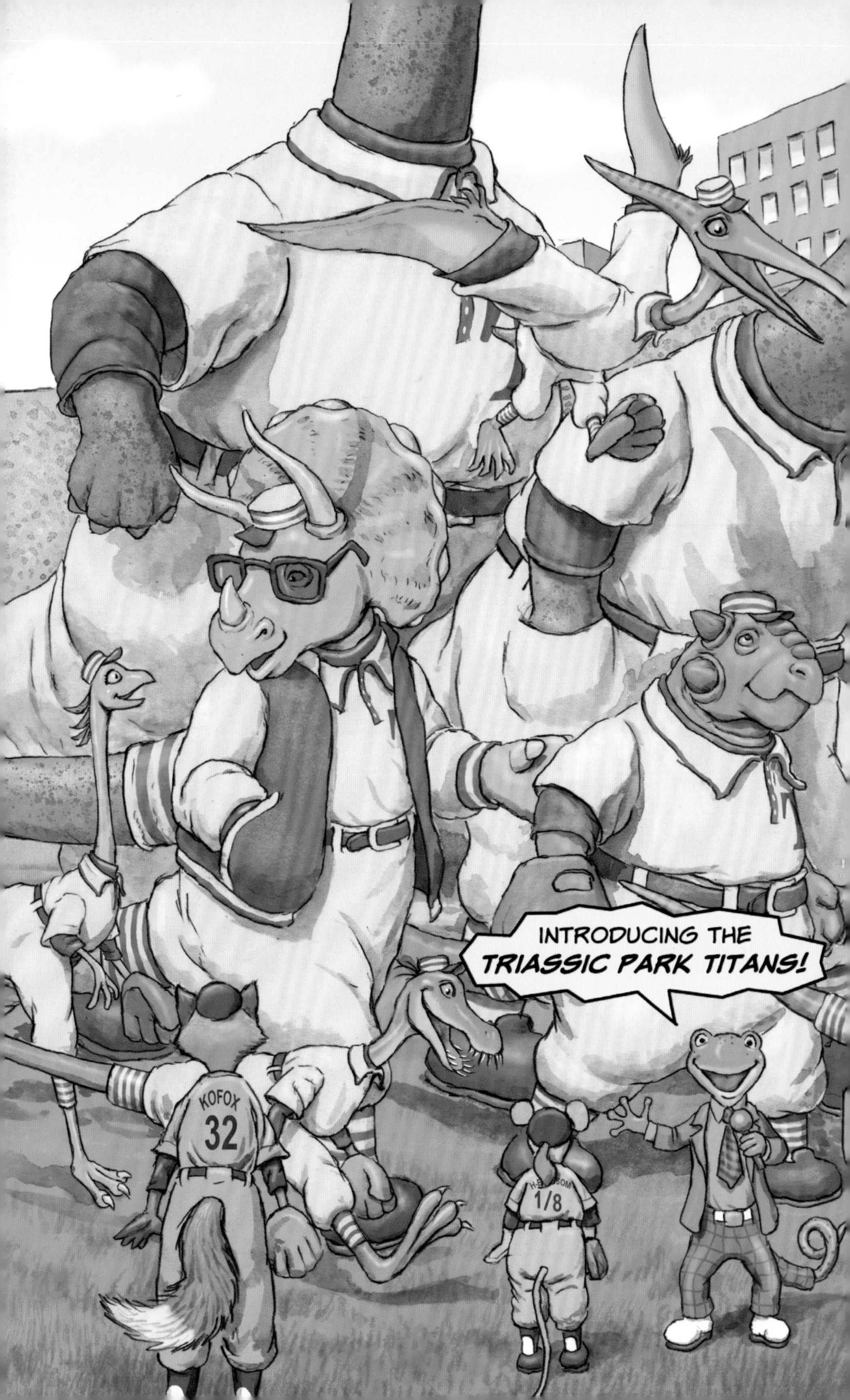
INTRODUCING THE TRIASSIC PARK TITANS!
KOFOX
32
1/8

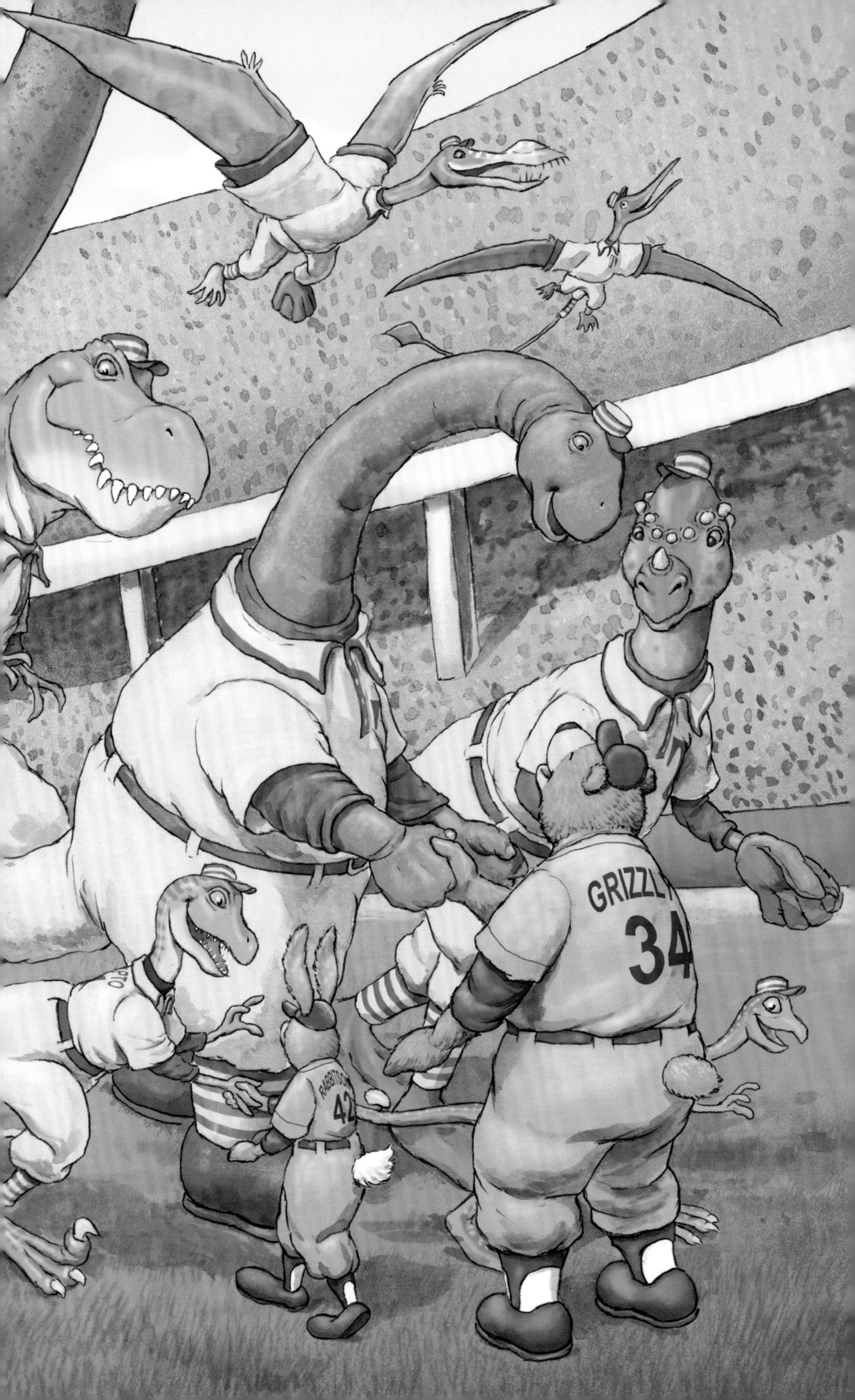
GRIZZL
34
42

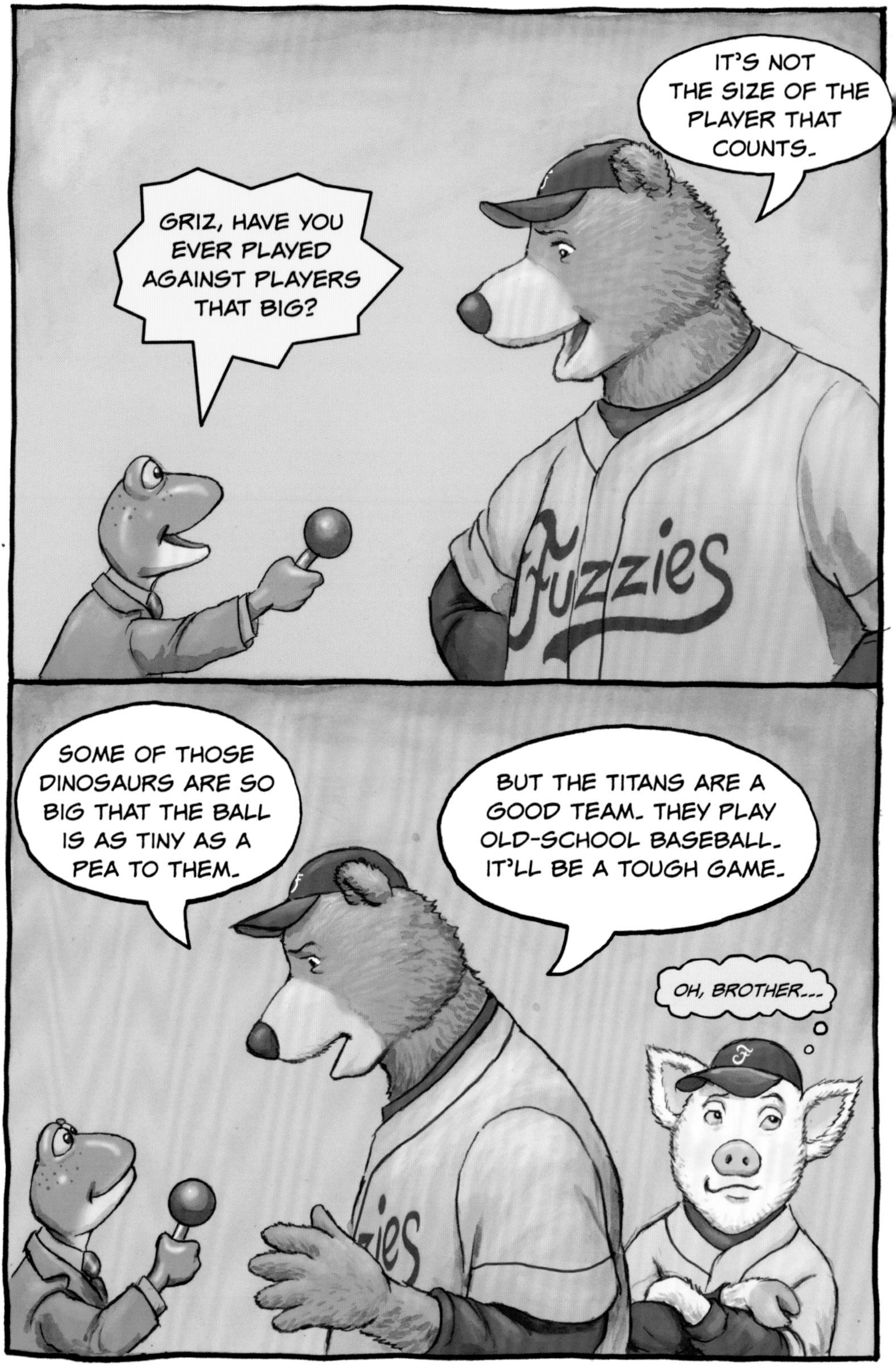
IT'S NOT THE SIZE OF THE PLAYER THAT COUNTS.
GRIZ, HAVE YOU EVER PLAYED AGAINST PLAYERS THAT BIG?
Fuzzies
SOME OF THOSE DINOSAURS ARE SO BIG THAT THE BALL IS AS TINY AS A PEA TO THEM.
BUT THE TITANS ARE A GOOD TEAM. THEY PLAY OLD-SCHOOL BASEBALL. IT'LL BE A TOUGH GAME.
OH, BROTHER...

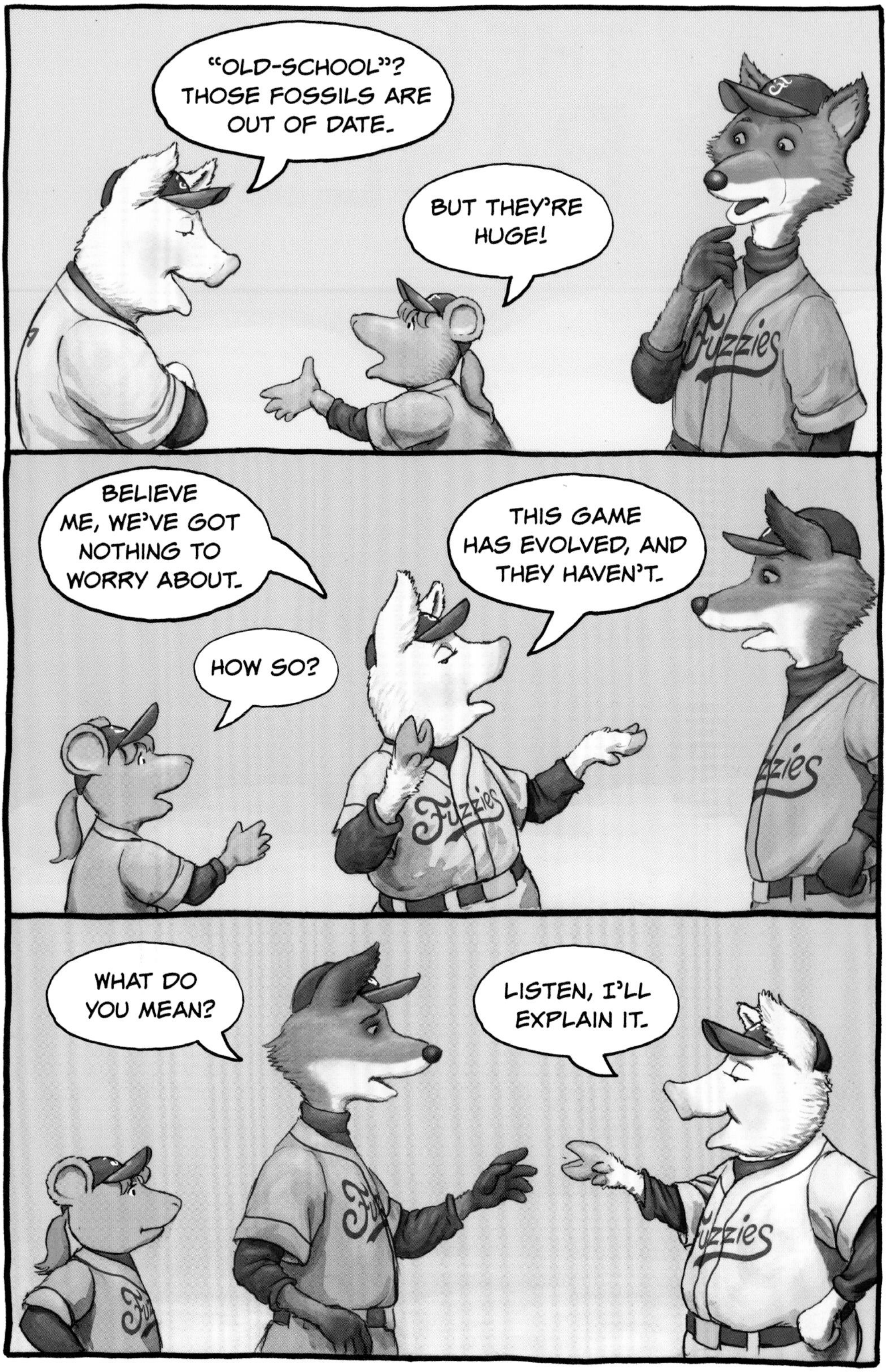
"OLD-SCHOOL"? THOSE FOSSILS ARE OUT OF DATE.
BUT THEY'RE HUGE!
BELIEVE ME, WE'VE GOT NOTHING TO WORRY ABOUT.
THIS GAME HAS EVOLVED, AND THEY HAVEN'T.
HOW SO?
WHAT DO YOU MEAN?
LISTEN, I'LL EXPLAIN IT.

HAMMY SOSA PRESENTS
THE HISTORY OF
BASEBALL

Baseball was invented during the **Handlebar Moustache Era**. The balls were carved out of dried moustache wax. The players all wore top hats. Batters stood on peach baskets and base runners rode on bicycles.

Don't miss all the rest in **FUZZY BASEBALL #4 "Di-No Hitters,"** available at booksellers and libraries everywhere!